Undead Hearts

by

Anakki Mayhem

Published in 2010

by

Malison Lexicon

ISBN 978-0-9807795-2-3

Printed in the USA by CreateSpace

The poem, La Vita Nuova, was written by Dante Alighieri,
(b1265-d1321, Florence, Italy) & is in the public domain.

This book is dedicated to all those curious minds
that ask the hard questions.
Much thanx to Ty Ambrose (Slam), Rachael Winn,
Monica Johansson, Dan Rogers, Miguel León,
John Munro & Robert Wilkinson for all the
inspiration & suggestions & karaoke stress
relief, & also to Ed Norton for being a muse
& giving me the time to write.
Many thanx also to Steve Kilbey, whose encouraging
words gave me the confidence to write book #2.

La Vita Nuova

In that book which is
My memory...
On the first page
That is the chapter when
I first met you
Appear the words...
Here begins a new life

by Dante Alighieri

Undead Hearts

The Beginning...

They got into Dante's 370Z in the triple garage. Larissa lay hidden in the back. Even for someone as small as she was, it was uncomfortably cramped. In case anyone saw him, it had to appear there was only one person in the car. Although the windows were tinted, they weren't so dark that inside became invisible. To be completely sure she was concealed, Dante and Kristof had thrown rugs over her and they left just after it got dark.

Dante had made a big show of not dealing with her supposed death. He hadn't been to uni at all in the four days since her disappearance. He spent his time either conspicuously sitting at the beach staring out to sea or hiding out in his house.

He preferred hiding out in his house because then he was actually with Larissa, but he was afraid that if he spent all his time in the house, her parents would feel as if they had to do something to get him out of there and inside the house was the only place Larissa was free for now. Her father only made the one visit to the house on that morning when he'd told of Larissa's disappearance. Between then and now, Dante had made sure to visit her family two or three times hoping that would mean Steve wouldn't come to their home again. It had worked, though seeing their pain tore him apart.

He'd boxed up both their surfboards and a freight company had called to collect them first thing in the morning. They were now on their way to his ranch in the USA. Just after they'd been collected, he'd made one last visit to her parents and brother, telling them he was dropping out and heading back home to England, and that he'd already shipped the boards ahead of him. They told him they understood. He felt bad deceiving them when they'd been so kind to him, trying to help him through his apparent grief while enduring their own, but there really was no alternative. This was the part of changing her he found the most difficult to cope with. It awoke all his own unresolved issues about his own family's loss.

He started the engine and pulled out of the driveway. Turning onto Beach Road, he followed it to Main South Road and then headed north to Cross Road. From there they were making their way to the South Eastern Freeway and the long drive to Melbourne. Dante could drive incredibly fast, and he liked to, but on this trip he wanted anyone who knew him or Larissa to see him leaving, so he stayed within the speed limit.

He drove until they were just past Tailem Bend, looking for an area with nothing nearby and no other traffic around them. Pulling over on the side of the road, he cut the engine so Larissa could get out and stretch. They'd fed well last night but Larissa still needed to drink a lot each day, so they planned for a hunt during their road trip.

Dante was constantly amazed that Larissa had taken to being a vampire without any difficulties. Every discovery of some new skill or ability she now had was greeted with excitement and wonder. Camille and Larissa had found they shared interests and became fast friends, something that helped Lari cope with her enforced confinement. Camille had even started teaching Larissa how to speak French. There had been a lot of hugs, sworn declarations of friendship forever, and promises to see each other again before Dante and Lari piled into the car for their big getaway.

Camille had chosen Lari's outfit for the journey, selecting a loose-fitting sheer black kaftan style top gathered at the waist that she layered over a black silk camisole and paired with black jersey harem pants and a pair of black platform heels that she'd bought for Lari as a going away present.

Dante got out and opened the passenger door and Lari leaped out, looking around before fixing her gaze on him, smiling. He was struck yet again by how feline she was and how easily she had fully embraced her vampire self. In her new clothes, with the changes that becoming a vampire had done, he was reminded again of her comment that they all appeared somehow young but ageless. He realized that he would think she was older than sixteen if he didn't know her age. Without warning, she had her arms around him and her lips against his.

"I love you, Dante Hill, and this is the beginning of our life together. Don't look so serious and worried. Everything is going to be fine."

He smiled at her optimism. "So you say, but we're not safely away yet. Tell me that when we're on the other side of the world." He kissed her and held her closer, sighing. "I love you far more than is probably good for me."

"Oh, you only just worked that out?" she laughed. "It's good I love you just as much then, isn't it?" She nuzzled him. "C'mon, let's get going. Further we drive, closer we are to where you feel safer."

"Okay." He kissed her once more and released her. She got into the passenger seat this time and he took the wheel again. He paused to smile at her as he started the engine. "I am looking forward to seeing the world through your eyes," he told her.

ONE

About an hour after they left Tailem Bend, she smiled and brushed Dante's face with her fingertips. His skin didn't feel cold and rock-like anymore now that hers was the same. The thirst was starting to make its presence felt, an irritating thought in her head that wouldn't go away. "Dante, when do we hunt and what about the flight? How long does it take to get to America?"

"We'll hunt in a little while. Keep your eyes and ears open for an opportunity. As for how long it takes to get to the States, well... It's about thirteen or fourteen hours on the plane plus the time we spend in airports. I think you should feed early in the morning, just before we go to the airport, and then you should be right till we get to America. We don't want you getting thirsty on the plane. That would be a little..." he searched for the right word.

"Awkward?" she asked.

"Yeah, awkward would describe it." He chuckled. "It'll be fine, Lari. If it becomes an issue, you can drink a little from me, although my blood won't actually make the thirst go away. You need human blood for that."

"Really? Then why were you all so worried I'd rip you apart to drink your blood when I was first made?"

"Because a newly made vampire simply wants blood and doesn't know that another vampire's blood won't help."

"Oh." She thought for a minute. "So why would I drink from you on the plane if I got thirsty then?"

"Because the act of drinking would help you to control the thirst until you could get somewhere safe to drink human blood."

"Okay, I get it. Thanks, Dante." She leaned across and kissed his cheek. "Hey, it could be our own version of the mile-high club!"

Dante looked at her with a startled expression, and then laughed. "Oh, beautiful. The vampire's mile-high club – a quick drink in an airplane toilet up in the skies!" He looked back at the road before she complained. He'd been astonished to discover that she still preferred him to watch the road, even though she knew a car accident wouldn't kill her now, and that his mental abilities and physical reflexes meant he could respond to any unexpected event incredibly fast. He glanced back at her, still laughing. "We are going to do that now, whether you're thirsty or not. The vamp's mile-high club starts on this flight."

She smiled at him. "Really? You're not making fun of me?"

"No, I love it. It's a great idea, Lari."

About an hour later they both sensed an opportunity to drink and he parked the car discreetly some distance away from their targets. Speeding silently through the night on foot, they found the sleeping campers and drank, returning to the car the same way.

At about four in the morning they found some more campers to drink from. Dante stood back and waited while Larissa fed from a few people, hoping to ensure she'd last the duration of the flight.

It was Larissa's first trip to Melbourne and she enjoyed the drive down the freeway into the city as the sun came up. She was thrilled to see the turn-off to the airport they'd be departing from later in the day.

Dante sold his car to a dealership in the city as soon as they arrived and hired a town car to take them and their few belongings back to Tullamarine Airport. The driver dropped them at the international departures terminal and they checked in, heading for the first class lounge immediately after. Lari was surprised to discover they were flying first class.

"Wow, Dante! My first trip overseas and it's in major style. You're awesome!" she planted a kiss on him.

He shrugged. "One of the benefits of a long life, Lari. Money is not an issue and we all prefer to fly first class. The confines of economy, and even business class, are a little more..." he raised an eyebrow and pulled a face, "for us."

"Oh," she answered. "I hadn't thought of that. Either of those things, actually. I guess it wouldn't be too much fun squished up in economy with humans, especially if I started to get thirsty." She frowned slightly. "Y'know, there's some part of my brain that knew you had money coz y'know, the car and the house and stuff, but I just never really thought about it, I guess."

"Ridiculous amount of money. You need never worry about it," he told her seriously.

"You're not joking, are you?" she asked him wide-eyed.

"No."

"Okay, Mr Moneybags, lead me astray."

He blinked, and then realizing she was teasing him, started laughing. "I love you, my beautiful witch. And I think I've already led you far enough astray."

Stopping in front of the concierge, Dante asked, "Hi, is it possible for us to have quick showers before our flight? We had a long drive here."

"Yes, sir. If you'd like to head towards our Day Spa, you'll find showers and towels."

"Thank you."

"Showers, Dante?" she asked him as they walked away.

"Yes. It's a long flight, Lari, and then a long drive. There are showers here so we might as well make use of them."

They followed the concierge's directions to the Day Spa where the attendant directed them to the showers. Ten minutes later they reunited at the entrance to the Day Spa.

"Feels good after a long drive to have a hot shower, doesn't it?" he asked her.

"Yeah, I'll give you that. It doesn't feel the same as when I was human, but it does feel good. Now where to?"

"How about the library?"

"Sure." Lari took hold of his hand again and they found the library, snuggling together in a comfortable lounge. "Oh, look! They've got playstations! Wanna play something with me?"

Dante laughed quietly. "Sure. I'll see the concierge and arrange it." He returned a few minutes later with a playstation and games.

They played for a while until Dante glanced at his watch and realized it was time for them to leave. With a cheeky grin, he told her, "C'mon Mrs Hill, time to go. Our flight will be boarding soon."

"Hey, you used a watch! I don't think I've ever seen you do that before," Larissa grinned back at him.

"I'm inside a large building. It's pretty hard to tell time inside a building without a watch and it's kind of important to keep track of time here," he laughingly told her.

Larissa laughed with him and waited by the lounge while he returned the playstation to the concierge. Dante made his way back to where Larissa was standing and took hold of her hand. Together, they strolled to the first class departure gate.

As they stepped on board the plane, Lari sent Dante a mental image of them naked and making love. He raised his eyebrows and looked at her.

"Naughty girl," he whispered to her with a grin. "Wait till we land."

TWO

Larissa had been impressed by the seats that could lay all the way down like a bed, but when the plane took off and she saw the ground falling away from her, she could barely contain her excitement. "Oh Dante, this is fantastic! I love flying! Can we do more of it?"

He smiled at her. "Yeah, we can do more." She sent him mental images of her snuggled up to him, nuzzling and kissing him, her hands brushing his face and throat. "I love you," he whispered to her seriously, knowing her acute hearing could hear the softest whisper.

"I love you, Dante. I'm so happy! I never knew I could be this happy. It's wonderful!" she whispered back, leaning across to touch his face with her fingertips.

One of the flight attendants told another, "Check out the lovebirds. How young and beautiful are they? Some people have all the luck."

"Young, beautiful and rich. This is first class," another answered.

Dante smiled and Larissa giggled, hearing what was inaudible to the rest of the passengers. "Behave and settle down, my wicked beauty. We're getting noticed and we don't want to attract attention," he admonished her, still smiling, his voice soft enough that only she could hear.

The flight was uneventful. They pretended to sleep for most of it, communicating silently and telepathically, timing their naps to coincide with when the meals were served. About halfway to Los Angeles, they got up and sneaked into the toilet together for their own version of the mile-high club, drinking a little from each other and giggling at their silliness.

About an hour before they were due to land, Larissa began to feel the nagging thirst. It began as an annoying thought that she couldn't make go away but within ten minutes of first feeling the desire for a drink, she became intensely aware of all the human bodies in the plane with her and her thirst escalated fast.

Reading her thoughts, Dante could feel her tension rising. Reacting quickly, he pulled her onto his lap and wrapping his arms around her, drew her close to him and discreetly offered her his wrist in a way that no-one was able to see her drinking from him. She drank quietly and fast, taking only enough to remove the edge from her thirst.

"You're right, Dante. It doesn't quench the thirst but it does make it more bearable. I'll be okay now," she told him in a voice too low for any human to hear. She stared deeply into his eyes, a half-smile playing across her face. Tracing the contours of his face tenderly with her fingertips, she whispered,

"I love you with all my heart," as she planted a lingering kiss on his lips before returning to her own seat.

The landing was as exciting to Lari as taking off had been. Once on the ground, they disembarked and made their way to baggage collection and then through immigration and customs.

Finally outside the terminal, Dante began looking around. He spotted a man standing next to a bright yellow Dodge Viper holding a placard that read "Hill".

"C'mon Lari. There's our car," Dante pointed toward the Viper. Taking her large overnight bag from her, and dragging his own suitcase with his other hand, he began walking toward the man with the placard. Lari looked lost for a moment and then, grinning, followed him to the car.

"Mr Hill?" the man asked.

"Yes. This is our car?" Dante replied, letting go of his suitcase and setting the overnight bag on the ground.

"Yes. My instructions were to deliver the car and keys to you here. All the car's papers are in order and are in the glovebox." He paused. "If you wouldn't mind showing me some identification, sir, I'll hand the car over to you and be on my way."

"Sure," Dante replied, pulling out his passport and showing it to the driver.

The man looked it over. "Thank you. Enjoy your stay in America."

"We will, thanks," Dante answered as the man smiled and walked away. Turning to smile at Lari, he asked, "Ready for your first road trip across America?"

"Oooooh, yes! Are we going all the way across America?"

He laughed as he tossed their bags into the boot. "No, the ranch isn't that far, but we can do it sometime, if you like."

Spontaneously, she hugged him. "I'd love that, Dante!"

"Did you know they call the boot a trunk here in America?" he asked her as he slammed the boot shut.

"No. Really? A trunk? Like an elephant," she giggled.

He smiled back at her. "Yeah, I don't think they mean like an elephant. More like in my time when the luggage we used to ship our things when travelling was usually called a trunk."

Lari stopped giggling and looked at him in wonder. "Was it really?"

"Yes, baby, it was."

"Wow," she absorbed the information. Dante opened the passenger door and she quickly jumped into the seat. "Dante, it feels weird sitting on this side of the car."

He got into the driver's seat. "Do you think you should be driving?" he smiled at her.

"Yeah, I don't think that would be very clever since I can't drive!" she laughed. Her laugh quickly changed to a frown as a group of tourists gathered near the car. "Oh, Dante... Can I get a drink soon, please? Or at least get me far away from people coz it's getting a bit unbearable again."

"On it, beautiful," he told her, starting the car and driving away.

THREE

He drove along the I-10 heading east towards New Mexico. It was mid-afternoon when they'd landed and Dante had told her it would be best to wait till dark before she fed, so they drove for hours, stopping only when the car needed fuel. Larissa stayed in the car with the windows up, waiting as Dante paid for the gas.

They were in Arizona by the time the sun was setting. "Can I drink now, Dante? I'm starting to go crazy here," she told him as they passed the sign welcoming them to Arizona.

"Yeah, baby, I'll pull over soon. I just don't want to stop anywhere there's too many people." Not much further along, he found a lay-by where a single camper van was parked. An elderly couple were sitting at a picnic table eating a leisurely early dinner. He parked the car a short distance from them.

"Okay. Lari, I know you're desperate for a drink but I want you to listen carefully. Drinking from people who aren't sleeping is much harder to do without getting caught when you're new like you are. I don't want to have to kill them, so please pay attention." He sighed. "It's just too early to hope to find someone sleeping and I can feel your thirst."

"Tell me what to do, Dante," she answered huskily, her eyes fixed on the couple.

"Approach them, smiling. Say hello and make polite conversation. You can only control one of them, so I'll handle the other for you. Stare into their eyes and do the same as if they were sleeping, but you must focus really hard. Don't lose concentration. And whatever you do, don't rush it. Some people will fall under your spell fast, but most take a bit longer when they're awake. Please be very careful."

"Will I drink from them here?"

"No, baby. We're going to convince them to get inside their camper and you'll drink from them both there. It's just a bit more discreet and safe if you feed in the van."

"Oh, okay. Now, Dante?"

"Now," he told her, getting out of the car. Dante waited for her to walk around the front of the car to join him before they walked together toward the couple. "Hi," he greeted the elderly couple, as he and Lari got closer.

"Hi there," the elderly American man answered, looking up at them. "Tourists?"

"Honeymooners," Dante told them. "Mind if we join you?"

"Not at all," invited the woman, patting the seat next to her.

Larissa sat beside the woman and Dante sat next to the man. "I'm Dante and this is my new bride, Larissa," he told them.

"Hello Dante and Larissa. I'm Ron and this is Margaret, my bride of going on forty years now," the elderly man replied, smiling.

His wife, Margaret, smiled at them both, "Hi there, dears."

"That's a nice van, Ron," Dante told the man, staring into his eyes.

"Yes, it's a Winnebago. Wife and I just retired and are heading south for winter." The man kept staring back at Dante, seemingly unaware that Dante was compelling him.

Margaret was looking at Dante and her husband, a slightly questioning expression on her face now. Larissa followed Dante's lead, capturing Margaret's attention. "Retired? You don't look old enough," she told her.

The woman instantly turned to face Lari, smiling. "Thank you, dear." She, too, was compelled to keep looking at Lari and unaware of the compulsion.

Dante continued staring into Ron's eyes. "How about you show me inside the van?"

"Yes. Come look inside the RV." Ron stood and Dante walked with him to the van.

"I'd love to see inside your RV," Larissa told Margaret, concentrating on compelling the woman to take them into the van.

"Let me show you inside, dear," the elderly woman replied, standing and walking to the van with Lari following. They all stepped inside and Lari closed the door behind them.

Ron was already reclining on the bed, asleep. Larissa instructed Margaret to join him and fall asleep, and then crouched over them, drinking first from the man and then his wife. Larissa was fascinated, as always, to see how her fang marks vanished so quickly and how easily she was able to convince them it was a dream and to forget both her and Dante.

It was finally dark when Lari and Dante slipped quietly out of the van. They cleaned up the campers' meal and locked up the van so that there was no evidence they'd ever been there before jumping into their car and speeding away into the night.

FOUR

Now that Larissa had fed and it was at last night, Dante picked up the speed and the miles flew by.

"You really do like driving fast, don't you?"

Dante glanced across at her and seeing her smiling face, answered, "Yup. I like doing nearly everything fast."

"I can think of one thing you don't do so fast," she giggled and tried to look sexy.

He grinned at her and shook his head. "Baby, you know I love you so don't start pouting," he said as he saw the sulky pout forming. "Are you trying to give me a hint?"

"No..." she looked thoughtful. "Although... we could if you wanted..."

"I always want," he told her, "but I think we'd do better to get to the ranch tonight."

"Can we get there tonight? Is it that close?"

"Well... technically, it should take us a bit longer but at the speed I'm driving and because I don't need sleep, we should make it before dawn."

"Oh. So how many miles is it? Everything is in miles here. I noticed."

"Yes, it is. And I'm not sure how many miles, but it's just outside Roswell in New Mexico."

"Roswell? Like where the aliens landed? Are you serious?" She looked incredulous. "You have a ranch just outside Roswell where aliens landed like, years ago? You, a vampire?" She giggled, then continued, "You weren't the aliens that landed, were you?"

He laughed. "No, I was not the aliens. And as far as I'm aware, if aliens did actually land there, they weren't vampires." He kept laughing. "Alien vampires, what next?"

"Hey, it's a good question." She frowned. "But, y'know, Dante... where do vampires come from? How do you know they didn't start out as aliens?"

He stopped laughing and glanced at her, a serious expression on his face. "Okay, I'm gonna pay that. I don't know where vampires came from, so maybe they were aliens that landed on earth a long time ago. I really don't know... But it would've had to be a lot before the 1940s. Vampires have been around for a lot longer than that... Kristof told me there are really ancient vampires that are thousands of years old." He looked briefly at Lari, seeing her wide eyes staring at him. "I haven't met any that old," he continued. "But I am pretty sure that it wasn't vampires that landed in Roswell back in the forties."

"Okay," she paused, looking out the window at the blurred scenery. "Were you there when it happened?"

"No, I was in Europe back then. I bought the ranch in the 1960s."

A few hours later, after they'd passed the sign welcoming them to New Mexico, they found another lay-by with a few cars and several RVs parked in the darkness. This time it was late enough that the people were all sleeping and Dante kept a look out while Lari slipped quietly into one of the vans to drink. Just as discreetly, she exited a short while later and rejoined him in the car.

"Better?" he asked her.

"Much, thank you. I should be all right for the rest of the drive now."

"Good. We'll head straight to the ranch now." He started the car and drove back onto the Interstate, heading towards New Mexico.

"I'm curious about something, Dante," Lari began as they sped along the road.

"What, beautiful?"

"Is it another myth that vampires need to be invited into a house?"

"No. That one's not a myth. But if there's no living owner, or the vampire owns the house, then an invite isn't necessary. You invited me into your house, so I could enter. Once a vampire's been invited, they don't need to be invited each time."

"Oh, I forgot about my house. I was wondering how I could get into those vans without needing to be invited."

"That's because they're not really a house. They're on wheels and they move. I'm not sure really how it works but I know that I... any vampire... can get in and out of them without needing to be invited. We don't need an invite into tents either. That's why we fed on campers on the way to the airport. It's just easier."

"And hotels? Do vampires need to be invited into hotels and motels? And what about rented houses?"

"For hotels and motels it's only if someone living has the room. Not into the lobbies or buildings in general. Rented places... well, as long as the person who rents the place invites you, then you can get in... I told you, I don't really understand how it works. I just know what I can and can't get into without an invite... more or less. Oh, and once you're invited in, you're always able to get in except for rented places. If the person who invited you stops renting the place, then you need a new invite from the new renter. Same with hotel and motels."

"Hmmmnnnnn..." Larissa stayed silent, looking deep in thought, but her thoughts were shielded so Dante couldn't read them. After they'd driven for another ten minutes, she spoke again, "Dante, how long before I don't need to drink so much?" She sighed. "I feel like I'm making things harder for you, needing to drink so often."

"Oh, Lari, don't feel like that. All of us went through that stage of needing so much blood, so frequently. You'll gradually need less, and I can't tell you when because it's different for each of us. Usually it takes a month or two for the feeding to lessen. And the older we get as a vampire, the less we seem to need to feed."

"Really? So, does that mean Kristof didn't need to feed as much as you coz he's heaps older as a vampire?"

"Yes. Where I feed every few days or so, he would feed about once a week."

"Wow." Larissa grew quiet, thinking about the new information. Dante looked across at her but didn't speak, letting her think things through. "So, those really ancient vampires... the ones that are thousands of years old... How often do you think they feed?"

Dante raised his eyebrows. "Your mind is amazing... The way you think always startles me." He thought about her question before answering. "I don't know, Lari. I would think that they don't feed very often. It could be that you reach a certain age as a vampire and the level you feed at stays the same from then on. I don't know. The oldest vampire I've ever met was a friend of Kristof's. He was only about fifty years older than Kris, and I didn't ask him about his feeding habits."

"Okay. I was just curious." Without hesitating, she continued, "Hey, Dante, where do you think those ancient vampires are?"

He looked at her with a slightly worried expression. "I don't know if your interest in them is a good thing. But, to answer your question, I think most of them are from Egypt or Mesopotamia, or from South America and I don't know where they actually are now."

"Egypt? Mesopotamia? South America?"

"Yes. That seems to be where the oldest stories of vampires come from."

"Oh."

"Forget about them, Lari. From the stories I've been told by other vampires, you don't want to meet them. They're not like us."

"Not like us? So others have met them?"

"Yes. Some have met them and they haven't described the meetings as pleasant. They have said that these ancients aren't like us at all. They are really very ancient. From a very different time in history and I don't think they mix with the human world at all. If they were ever human, they've long since forgotten it. They just feed from this world."

"Oh." She leaned across to Dante and smiled as her head brushed his shoulder. "Don't look so worried, Dante. I'm not about to go looking for them. I'm just curious."

"Good." He smiled back at her. "New subject, please."

FIVE

The miles sped by and eventually they were driving down a narrow road in New Mexico that seemed somehow spooky and gothic with tall trees lining either side.

"Y'know, Dante, this seems like an appropriate place for a vampire hideout," Lari told him, her eyes eagerly taking in the scenery.

"Does a bit, doesn't it?" he smiled. "We're nearly there." A few minutes later as the sun began to hint of rising, he slowed the car and pulled into a concealed driveway.

"Neat! I wouldn't have known that was there!"

"Yes, you would've seen it if you'd been looking, but a human would find it harder to spot," he corrected her.

"Oh." Her eyes grew wider as they wound their way through the dense trees lining the driveway and finally came to a stop in front of a sprawling white weatherboard two-storey Queen Anne style house. "This is it?" she asked him.

"Yes. Do you like it?"

"Oh, yes! It's kind of gothic and sort of what I'd imagine being the kind of house you should own. I bet it's got high ceilings and huge rooms, too. Does it have chandeliers?" Without waiting for him to answer, she leapt out of the car and raced to the front door. "Dante?" she called out, spinning round to face him.

He joined her, smiling and waving a key in front of her. Unlocking the door, he stepped aside to let her run in. The big entry held a wide sweeping staircase leading to the next floor and a big arch dividing the entry from the front parlour where furniture covered in white sheets and a thick layer of dust over everything including the wooden floorboards could be seen. Closed doors concealed the rest of the rooms. Quickly she raced through all the downstairs rooms, opening all the doors, while he waited by the entrance. A beautiful but dusty crystal chandelier hung in the large front room.

"Oh, Dante! This is awesome! And it does have a chandelier! How long are we gonna stay here?"

"I hadn't decided that, but I'm glad you like it." He smiled as she raced up the staircase to explore the upper level. While she was looking around, he took their bags from the car and brought them inside. He was just shutting the front door as she returned downstairs.

"Tell me one thing, Dante..." she paused, standing on the bottom step, one hand still holding the banister.

"Yes?"

"You said we don't sleep... Well, except that once every few years we need to have some sort of rest thing... And since I became a vampire, I haven't slept or wanted to... So, if this has been your house since the 1960s, how come there are beds in all the bedrooms?"

"Oh, that's because I had humans looking after this place while I lived here and after I left it and it would've seemed strange to them if there were no beds in the bedrooms, so when I bought this place, I had beds put into all the bedrooms. They've never been slept in." He frowned slightly. "Well, not that I know of. The humans looking after this place might've used them, but I doubt it. How come you never asked about the beds in Kristof's house?"

"Coz I guess I never thought about it then... and besides we used one of those beds to make love," she paused and continued before he could interrupt, "and you said you never had a vampire girlfriend or a human girlfriend since you became a vampire until you met me, so you shouldn't have been using them for that if you were telling me the truth! Ha!" She laughed and poked her tongue out at him.

"No, there were no other girlfriends... you're my one and only." He paused and grinned cheekily, "Well, I think it's time one of these beds saw some use then."

"Ooooh, promises!" She grinned back at him and then glanced around at the dust. "So, where are they now? The humans? Coz it seems very dusty for somewhere that people have been looking after."

"I left here over thirty years ago. The people I hired to look after the place are long gone now." He looked thoughtful. "It must be more than twenty years since anyone came through and cleaned here."

Lari tilted her head as she looked at him, wondering. "Why didn't you keep it looked after?"

"I wanted it to fade from people's memories, so I could return and use it again and not have people remember that I used to live here."

"Oh, so you can do that now?"

"I don't know. We're here much earlier than I planned to come back. There may still be people who remember me from before. We should probably be very careful about being seen while we work things out."

"All right. So we should at least clean up this place coz we are staying here for a while, aren't we? Please say we are..."

He smiled at her. "Yes, baby, we're staying here a little while. I don't know how long for, though. I hadn't thought it through that much yet. Anyway, Roswell's a great place to explore. I really enjoyed my first time here. And this is also a good base for us to travel from. After all, you've never been to America before, so it's all new for you."

"Oh, are we going to travel more? And wait... I know something I want to see here before we go elsewhere... It's Roswell where there's an alien museum, isn't it?" Dante nodded, and Lari continued, "Oooooh, I want to go see that. Can we go there?"

"Yes. But before we go roaming about town, I want to make sure it'll be okay for me to be seen about. It's no problem for you to go looking around because you've never been here before, but if anyone I knew from all those years ago is still here and they see me... well, it might be a problem."

"I don't want to go by myself, Dante. I want to see these things with you." She pouted at him.

He smiled. "I know, baby. Tonight we'll head into town so I can do some eavesdropping on people's thoughts... You'll want to feed by then, too. I wouldn't mind feeding tonight, either. Travel can be draining."

"Especially when your beloved uses you as in-flight drinks," she laughed, leaping off the stairs and hugging him.

"Yes, especially then," he laughed with her, kissing her lips.

"Where else are we going to go, Dante?" she asked in between kisses.

"Tell you later," he answered, picking her up and carrying her to the master bedroom. "I have other things in mind right now," he told her, sending her the same mental image she'd given him as they boarded the plane in Australia.

"Oooh, Dante! Yes, please!"

Together, they ripped the dusty covers from the bed and tore the clothes from each other in a blur of speed. Her legs wrapped around his hips, drawing him into her and they made love in a frenzy of desire. She gouged her fingers into his back and sunk her teeth into him as he bit into her and they both reached orgasm drinking from each other.

SIX

Late that night they slipped into town on foot, quietly walking the streets unnoticed. Dante led her towards a home near the local library where he paused in the shadows, listening.

Lari waited quietly beside him. She didn't know whose conversations he was listening to, so she blanked all the conversations out of her mind and thought about how much her life had changed in a little over a week and how it seemed as if much more time had passed.

"Lari," Dante's voice interrupted her train of thought.

"Yes?" she whispered back.

"It should be okay for us to go for a wander around town tomorrow. We can see that museum, if you like."

She looked at the house. "Is this where someone you knew lived?"

"Yes. But they don't live here anymore. It belongs to strangers who only moved to Roswell a few years ago and bought the house as a deceased estate."

"That's a good thing?" she asked.

"Yes," he paused. "And no. I'm sad that my friends have died but relieved that we can walk about town."

"Aren't there other people you're worried about recognizing you?"

"No. Jean's family is the one that looked after my house when I lived here and after I left. I was never really close to anyone else here."

"Jean?"

"Yes. Jean Thomas was my housekeeper and Bernie, her husband, was the groundskeeper and gardener. I wonder what happened to them." He stared up at the house thoughtfully. "They were probably in their fifties when I left, so perhaps it was just old age."

"Well, if it was a deceased estate a few years ago, and they were fifty-something when you left, then they must've been in their eighties by the time it became a deceased estate."

"Yeah. Though I doubt they both died of old age at the same time. So either one had already died or they had some kind of accident."

Lari gave him a hug. "You can find out, can't you? Or would that be awkward?"

"Maybe. I'd have to be very cautious and discreet." He hugged her. "Doesn't really matter anyway. I'm just a bit curious. They were my friends a long time ago."

"What about kids? Didn't they have any?"

"Yeah, I think they had a son. I never met him. He was already an adult by the time I hired Jean and Bernie and he lived in another state. They used to vacation with him, I think." He smiled at Lari. "C'mon, let's be tourists and take a walk around town. You can point out things other than the alien museum that you want to look at."

"Cool. I can tell you now, though, that it's number one on my list!"

He laughed. "You'll like it. It's pretty good." They began walking back toward the main street.

"Oh, have you been already?" she asked, a hint of disappointment in her voice.

"No, I haven't actually. But Kris has, and he took tons of photos and told us all about it. He and Lucy came over last year for a brief visit."

"Did they? Like a holiday?"

"Yes. They were only in the US for a couple of weeks."

"Why didn't they stay in your house?"

"I didn't know they were going to Roswell, and besides, they were only in town for a couple of days."

"Why were they here?"

"Anniversary."

"Oh, that's romantic!" Lari frowned. "What anniversary? Are they married? Or did you mean the anniversary of when they got together or something else?"

"Anniversary of when they married the first time."

"The first time? How many times have they gotten married?"

"A few." He grinned. "They like doing it – the wedding thing. So they pretend to be girlfriend and boyfriend for a while and then they get engaged and have a spectacular wedding and then usually not long after that they take off and move."

"Oh." Lari smiled. "That sounds like fun. We could do that too, y'know."

"Maybe one day." He shook his head at her. "Why are you in such a rush to do everything? You have forever now, you know. Besides, according to your passport, you're already Mrs Hill."

Lari thumped him lightly. "Hahaha! Not fair. I want the wedding too!"

They both laughed and he slipped his arm around her waist, pulling her closer to him. "One day. I promise."

They walked in silence along the quiet main street. Dante pointed out the alien museum and Lari was enchanted by the images of aliens plastered all over the town. Outside the Denny's, Lari whispered to Dante, "Hey, we are going to feed tonight, aren't we? Coz I think I can feel the thirst coming on."

"Yeah, baby. Let's head for some camping grounds I know of."

"Sounds good." They changed direction and in unison, sped up so that they seemed to just disappear, turning east onto Route 380 and then south onto NM409, not slowing down until they reached Bottomless Lakes State Park. "Here?" Lari asked Dante.

"Yes," he whispered in reply. "Find some campers in tents that aren't crowded together." He paused and looked serious. "Lari, one thing... If ever anyone around here should think they recognize me or say I remind them of the Dante who used to live here in the sixties, just tell them I'm the namesake grandson who inherited the old house and came to check it out. Okay?"

Lari turned and looked at him thoughtfully. "Are you still worried it might happen?"

Dante shrugged and gave her a wry grin. "Maybe not, but I've stayed under the radar all these years because I'm extra careful."

"Well, don't worry. If it happens, then that's what I'll say." She frowned slightly as she looked at Dante's worried expression. "I mean it. Don't worry. Anyone who knew you back then will believe you're a lookalike grandson. Trust me. People don't automatically think you're a vampire or that people who look like someone from thirty-something years ago must be the same person. You only think like that coz you know vampires exist. Most people don't think that way." She smiled at him. "Now can we feed? I can smell the blood."

Dante smiled. "Okay, I won't worry so much. C'mon, let's feed." They split up and disappeared into the dark tents, feeding quietly and unobserved, meeting back at the entrance to the park a short while later.

"Home, Dante, or shall we explore a bit?" Lari asked him.

"Why don't we go for a run and explore a bit? Since it's all new for you and I wouldn't mind having a look around and seeing how it's changed."

"Sure," she answered. "Lead the way." He took her hand and together they disappeared into the darkness, running silently through the night.

SEVEN

Two days after their arrival in Roswell, Dante offered to take Lari to visit the alien museum in town.

"Can I get a camera to take photos? You said Kristof took heaps of photos so we are allowed to take photos there, aren't we?" she asked him.

"Sure we can, baby," he smiled at her. "There's a Walmart in town. We can stop there first and buy you a camera. Did you want a digital still camera or a video camera?"

"Oooh... I hadn't thought of that... Ummnnn... Can I have both?" she smiled at him. "Please," she added.

Dante laughed. "Of course you can." He frowned slightly. "You can use my Macbook to upload your pictures to."

"Dante, you're brilliant! I can email some to Camille! Thank you!" she squealed, throwing her arms around his neck. "Why are you frowning?"

"I was just thinking that you should have your own computer."

"Why? Don't you like sharing yours with me?"

"I don't mind. I just thought you'd like to have your own."

"Ok. Buy me one then. One like yours, please, coz I like yours." She released her grip on him and stepped back, looking thoughtful. "Dante?"

"Yes, baby?"

She paused. "Doesn't matter." Lari smiled at him again. "Are we ready to go? Are we going to drive into town? We should, I guess, since it's daytime."

"Yes, and yes. Come on... To Walmart first and then to the museum." He put his arm around her shoulder and together they started to walk to the front door. "Hey, I just realized... You've never been to a Walmart!"

She stopped walking and gave him a look that said she thought he'd gone mad. "It's a department store, right?"

"Yeah, sort of... but nothing like you've ever seen in Australia.... Some of them are almost like towns in themselves..."

"You're kidding, right?" she asked.

"Nope."

"Wow." Lari stared at him for a minute and then slipping her hand into Dante's, resumed walking to the door. "Well, let's go then. I'm kinda curious about this store now, too."

Dante laughed and walked with her to the car. They drove into town and Lari started laughing as soon as they parked the car in front of the store. "There's an alien on the store!" she exclaimed. "Oh, I never noticed it before, Dante!

It's just great! After we've bought my cameras, I'm going to take a photo of that!"

Dante grinned back at her. "I knew I was going to love seeing the world through your eyes," he told her.

Once inside the building, Lari was impressed by the size of the store. "You're right... it's huge."

"This one's actually small compared to some I've seen," he told her. "Let's find the cameras, okay?"

"Sure... but I can look around a bit too, can't I?" she asked.

He shook his head in disbelief. "Yeah, sure you can... Was there something in particular you wanted to look at?"

"No, just random stuff I guess..."

Dante laughed. "Okay, let's look around while we look for the cameras."

Nearly an hour later, with her cameras in hand, they reached the alien museum. "Dante!" she squealed, "This is brilliant! I've got to get some photos of this!" She quickly started snapping pictures of the outside of the building. "Look, it's called the International UFO Museum and Research Center! What a name! That's so cool!" Switching to her new video camera she panned across the building making sure to capture Dante in her footage. He smiled at her excitement and waited till she was done. She handed him the video camera. "You can be video man and I'll take the photos. How's that sound?"

"Sounds good to me," he answered. "Ready to go in now?"

"Yup." She took his hand and they entered the museum. Once inside, she raced across to one of the displays. "Oh, Dante, look at this!" she exclaimed. Immediately she started taking more photos and reading the information, taking her time to look at each display intently. Dante followed her, taking video footage of Lari and the museum displays.

It took them a little over an hour to wander through the museum and Lari was fascinated by all the displays and the information they contained. Finally reaching the gift shop at the end, she almost ran into it, selecting a handful of souvenirs for Dante to purchase for Camille, Cristóbal, Kristof and Lucy. "Do you think they'll like these, Dante?" she asked him.

"Yeah, I'm sure they will. Are we going to wrap and post them today?"

"Yes, please." She chose another two more souvenirs. "I want these for us to remember today."

"I'll remember today without the need for souvenirs, but thank you anyway, my beautiful witch. Which one is for me?"

Lari waited till he'd paid for all the items and then as they were leaving, she pulled the souvenir she'd chosen for him from the bag. "The pappa alien is yours," she told him as she handed a ceramic alien figurine to him. "I get the green bendy one."

"Thank you." He leaned down to kiss her. "I love you, beautiful, and I love my souvenir."

EIGHT

About a week after their arrival in Roswell, Larissa heard a knock at the front door. Wondering who would be visiting them when they knew no-one and nobody knew they were there, she went to the front room to peek through the curtains.

Immediately she got excited as she realized it was someone from the freight company with their surfboards. She raced to the door and flung it open.

"Hi," she greeted the delivery guy.

"Hi, is there a Dante Hill here?" he asked.

"Yeah, I'll just get him," she told him. Turning to face inside, she called loudly, "Dante! There's someone at the door to see you!" She turned back to the delivery guy. "He'll just be a minute."

"This is a hard place to find," the delivery guy told her. "I think I must've driven past the entrance two or three times before I realized it was there."

"Yeah, it can be hard to spot if you've never been here before," she answered.

"Who wants to see me?" Dante asked her telepathically.

"Come see," she answered silently, enjoying herself.

"Witch!" he retorted silently, as he appeared in the hallway behind her.

"Dante Hill?" the delivery guy asked as he saw him.

"Yes," Dante answered.

"I have two packages here for you if you'd just sign for them, sir," the man pointed at the boxed up surfboards beside him and offered him a clipboard that held a form and a pen.

"Sure," Dante answered as he opened the screen to take the clipboard and scrawled a signature on the form.

"Thank you, sir. Goodbye." The delivery guy retrieved his clipboard from Dante and gave them a brief wave as he returned to his van, jumping in and taking off immediately, disappearing into the trees down the long drive.

"Dante! It's our surfboards! They're here!" Lari ran out onto the porch and grabbed a box. Dante joined her and picked up the second box. They went back into the house and immediately Lari began tearing open the packaging.

"Oooh, I have your board! That means you must have mine."

"Well, I'll let you open it then, Miss Excitement," he laughingly told her.

"Thank you." She began to tear open the second package revealing her own board. "Oh, I've missed my board!" she exclaimed. "And I miss surfing. Where can we surf, Dante? And when can we go there?" She pouted at him.

"You wouldn't let me surf in Australia after I became a vampire."

"No, that wouldn't have been a smart thing to do."

"I could've gone somewhere far from home, y'know..."

He shook his head. "I think I remember having this conversation in Australia."

"Well, we're not in Australia anymore and my board is here and I want to surf. So, where and when can we go surfing?"

"Not here in Roswell... no waves." He chuckled.

"Oh, you smartarse!" Lari leapt up and thumped him lightly. "Tell me where we can go surfing and when we can go there or I'll thump you harder!"

He laughed. "I could really stretch this out, couldn't I?"

"Dante! I'll chuck a tantrum!" She stamped her foot and pouted at him, folding her arms and frowning fiercely.

He laughed harder. "Oh no, not a tantrum... Please, no tantrum..." He kept laughing. "Oh baby, I can't do it... I give in, and you can stop pouting. We can go surfing in Northern California. That's not really that far from here. Not for us. I don't know the when, though. Okay?"

"Why don't you know when? Why can't we just go surfing now?"

"I know it doesn't seem like it here coz the weather's pretty good, but it's winter, y'know... It snows in lots of places. Wouldn't you like to try skiing or something? Besides, did you see my car? I don't know where a couple of surfboards would fit in it."

"Oh," she paused. "I don't want to go skiing. I want to surf." She thought about it for a minute. "Well, maybe one day I wouldn't mind trying skiing, but I wanna surf before I try that. And I forgot about the car. So how will we get our surfboards to Northern California? Will we run with them?"

"There's a thought, but no, I had something else in mind."

"What?"

"Would you like to learn to drive, Lari?"

"Me? You would teach me? Will I get a licence too?"

"Yes, I'll teach you to drive and buy you a car that can carry surfboards and you can get a licence here I think. I'll have to check that last one. But if you can't actually get a licence, I'll get you one the same way you got a passport. Is that okay with you?"

"Oh yeah! I'd love that Dante! That's such an awesome idea! And can I have a Hummer?" She threw her arms around him and showered him with kisses.

"A Hummer?" he asked in between kisses.

She stopped kissing him, but kept her arms around his neck. "Yeah, I like them. I always thought I'd like to have one some day."

"Okay, a Hummer it is then. Any particular colour you prefer?"

"Blue. Do they come in blue?"

"I don't know, beautiful, but if they don't we'll have it custom painted blue for you."

"Oh, I love you Dante! I love you! I love you! I love you!" She danced around him, punctuating each sentence with a kiss. "When do I start my driving lessons?"

"How about today? You can learn in the Viper. But no licence and no Hummer until you can really drive."

She raced out to the car, "Come on then, lessons start now!"

Dante laughed as he followed her out, speaking softly to himself, "What have I done? The roads will never be safe again..."

NINE

Two days later and Lari could finally drive down the driveway without stalling the Viper or bunny-hopping. She still hadn't mastered gear changes and her acceleration and braking techniques were kind of sudden and not at all smooth, but at last they were making progress. She stopped suddenly as they reached the gate.

"Clutch!" Dante called out as the car lurched and stalled.

"Oops, sorry, I forgot again," she smiled sheepishly. "Can you get automatic Hummers? Coz maybe we should think about that... I don't know if I'll ever get the hang of gears."

"No. Well, I don't know if you can or not, but you're going to learn gears before I'm giving you a car coz the Viper has gears and I'm not buying you a car until you can drive." He leaned over and kissed her. "You'll get there, beautiful. You've only been learning for two days."

She sighed. "Yeah, I guess so. I didn't think it was going to be this hard."

"Okay. Do you want to try turning around or do you want me to do it again?"

"You do it."

"There's no traffic..."

"Yeah, but I bet the minute it's me out there on that road, there'll be a heap of traffic just waiting to collide with me." She grinned at him and got out of the car.

"If you say so," he laughed, getting out and walking round to hop in the driver's side. "Oh, you could've put the seat back for me!" he told her as he squeezed in and moved the seat back.

"Nah, it's more fun watching you struggle to get in when it's all the way forward," she laughed. "No, I'm sorry, really I am, I forgot to do that too." Lari remained standing on the side of the drive as he drove out onto the road to turn the car around and pulled up next to her in the driveway. Quickly, Lari hopped into the passenger side.

"You're not going to drive us back to the house?" he asked.

"Nope. I'm done for now. I need a break from gears and clutches and stuff."

"Okay." He drove back up the long drive and parked in front of the house. "There's no deadline you know, beautiful..."

"Yeah, I know Dante. I just don't know if I'm cut out for driving. I can't get the hang of gears and doing the clutch and the brake and the accelerator. It's like I've got to do too many things at the same time."

"You will get the hang of it. Listen, surfing isn't that easy and you're an amazing surfer. It takes balance and coordination. You don't need balance to drive – just the coordination, and you have that. You've just got to learn the things you need to coordinate, and you will."

Lari smiled at him. "You're comparing driving to surfing? There's something really wrong with that comparison only I'm not sure what it is yet."

"Don't think too hard about it. Just remember the part where I said you already have the coordination you need to drive. You just have to learn what you need to coordinate and when. Okay?"

"Okay." She leaned over and rested her head on his shoulder. "Is there a fast way to learn what I have to coordinate?"

"Sorry baby, but I think the answer to that is no. You're just going to have to practice and practice until you get the hang of it."

"Uggh... Learning to drive really isn't as much fun as it sounds."

He laughed softly. "It gets better. In about a week, you'll like it more. Think about this too, beautiful... If you were still human it could take you months to learn to drive but coz you're a vampire now and don't need to sleep or go to school or things like that, and you can practice as much as you want, whenever you want, you'll learn to drive in only a few weeks."

"That still sounds like a lot of learning."

"But in just a few weeks time you could be driving your very own first car... a great big blue Hummer..."

"Mmmmnnn..."

"With our surfboards on the roof, on our way to a beach in California where we can go surfing..." he continued, trying to reignite her desire to learn to drive.

"Okay, you win. I want to go surfing and apparently there won't be a Hummer to transport our boards unless I can drive it, so I'm gonna keep learning to drive."

TEN

Two weeks after she started learning, Lari was finally getting the hang of driving. "So, Dante... am I going to drive anywhere other than our driveway or am I stuck here forever?" she asked him as they got into the Viper parked at the front of the house.

"You ready to take on the roads?" he asked with a half-smile.

"Yeah... well... yeah, I have to do it sometime, don't I?"

"You do, indeed. How about we head down some quiet roads around here until you feel a bit more confident? Then we can try a bit of traffic."

"Really? Now?" she asked, her eyes wide.

"Yes, now. Turn right when you get to our gate and then take the first road on the left."

"Okay..." She sounded uncertain as she started the car and steered it down the drive. Lari came to a stop at the gate, checking the road for traffic before making a right turn onto the road.

Dante's eyes grew wide. "Baby, don't panic, but you're on the wrong side of the road. They drive on the left side here, so can we swap sides of the road before something comes the other way?"

Lari looked at him horrified and quickly switched sides of the road. "Sorry, I forgot about that. If I still had a heartbeat, Dante, it'd be going triple time right now." Staying on the correct side of the road now, she drove for nearly a mile till she came to a crossroad. Slowing almost to a stop, she carefully made a left-turn into it, making sure she wasn't turning onto the wrong side of the road. "Now where, Dante?" she asked as they drove along the empty country road.

"Well, first thing, you can speed up. The speed limit is seventy and you're barely doing thirty, I think."

"It seems too fast," she told him, pulling a face and gripping the steering wheel as she accelerated.

"You're doing fine. This road goes for miles so don't worry that you're going to need to brake for a while yet."

"What if something runs out onto the road?"

"Like what?"

"Ummmnn... a rabbit? Or a deer? Or whatever wild animals it is they have around here..."

"Your reflexes are way faster than a human's, Lari. You'll hit those brakes faster than you think you can." He paused and smiled. "But I don't think any wild animals are going to run out in front of you."

"Really? You don't? What makes you think that?" she asked, still intently studying the road and clutching the steering wheel.

"They heard I was taking you out on the roads today and they're all hiding." He laughed gently.

She flicked her eyes from the road to glare briefly at him. "That's not funny," she told him. "When we get home, I'm gonna hurt you."

He laughed again. "I'm sorry, beautiful. Please don't hurt me."

"Well... don't be mean then," she laughed. "So do I just follow this road till it ends?"

"No, in about four or five miles, you'll see a road on your left. Turn there."

"Is this like a big block or something?"

"You could say that. You'll drive down that road for about three miles and take another road on your left and drive down that one for about six miles till you come back to our road. Turn left again and drive till you see our gate and then you can either turn right into it or we can do your 'big block' again, if you want."

"I'll let you know when we get there." The crossroad loomed in front of her. "This is where I turn, Dante?"

"Yes, beautiful. Left turn here."

She slowed down and made the turn, speeding up as soon as the turn was completed.

"You're getting better at it already, beautiful," he told her. "Though I love that frown of concentration as you turn a corner."

"Watch it, Dante... no jokes at my expense or I'm gonna hurt ya," she laughed. He joined in the laughter. "So, how goes the licence thing? What if I get stopped or something coz I don't have a permit, do I?"

"Don't worry about it. We're very unlikely to get stopped out here, and if it does happen that we do get stopped, either you or I can compel the officer to believe it never happened."

"If you say so," she sounded doubtful. "This where I turn?" she asked as another crossroad loomed.

"Yes," he told her. "Don't worry. I don't think it's going to happen out here, though I will have to give some thought to driving in town before we do that."

"This is getting easier, Dante," she told him, her grip on the steering wheel easing.

"Good."

She reached a stop sign and came to a halt, waiting for a truck to pass before turning left again. "Oh, that was our gate!" she exclaimed as they drove past it. "Guess we're doing another lap!"

ELEVEN

Another couple of weeks passed and Lari got better at driving. Dante arranged for her to have a permit and they started driving into town a week after her first time on the roads. It was the week between Christmas and New Year so there weren't many other vehicles on the road her first time driving into town, but the traffic lights and pedestrians made her nervous. It was only now that she was starting to feel more confident about her driving. So far no-one had pulled them over to check her permit either.

Yesterday they'd driven mostly down the country roads, exploring further around their new home and today she was looking forward to another trip into the town centre.

"Dante!" she called as she scooped the car keys from the hall table. "I want to practice my driving. Where are you, Dante?" She paused at the doorway, a slight frown creasing her forehead. "Dante?" Her frown deepened and she spun around to walk back into the house. "Where is he?" she muttered to herself.

She checked the ground floor and couldn't find him anywhere. "Dante?" she called again, pausing at the back door. "Maybe he's out here..." she told herself as she walked outside. "Hey, Dante! I want to practice driving. Where are you?" she called again as she wandered into the backyard. He wasn't anywhere to be seen in the empty backyard so she went back inside and made her way to the front door. "I know he's not upstairs coz that's where I was, so he must be out here," she muttered as she walked out the front door. "Dante!" she called again, coming to a stop at the top of the porch stairs.

The Viper was parked out front where she'd left it the day before but there was still no sign of Dante anywhere. "Are you ignoring me? You can't be so far away that you can't hear me... can you?" she began to wonder out loud.

She was staring down the drive, looking puzzled, when she heard an engine that sounded like it was coming towards her. "What?" she asked out loud as she saw a slate blue metallic Hummer travelling up the drive. It pulled up behind the Viper and Dante jumped out.

"Baby, is it what you wanted?" he called out to her.

"Oh Dante! Is that where you've been? I wondered why I couldn't find you. It's for me, isn't it?" she exclaimed, leaping off the porch and running into his open arms.

"Yes, it's for you," he laughingly told her as she showered him with kisses. "Congratulations. Today you have a licence." He slipped out of her grasp and reached into his pocket to remove a licence and hand it to her.

"Oh! I have a licence! That's so cool, Dante! Thank you so much!" She took the licence from him and studied it briefly before throwing herself at him again. "Damn, you can keep a secret! You must've been organizing that for ages!"

"Only a week," he told her. "Want to take your new Hummer for a drive?"

"Oh yes! I do! But wait!" Lari disappeared into the house, returning a few minutes later clutching her camera. "I locked the house up and I want pictures first!" she told him as she ran around the Hummer taking photos. "There, done!" She quickly leapt into the vehicle, waiting for Dante to jump into the passenger side and handing him the camera.

"Are you going to start it and take us somewhere?" he asked her when she sat and just stared at the dash.

"Ummnnn... Dante... I didn't realize it would be so big. It seems much bigger than the Viper."

"It is bigger, but driving is the same. You just need a bit more room for this than you do with the Viper." He paused, "And I don't think this corners as well but since you're such a slow driver, that won't matter to you." He laughed softly.

"Ooooh, you!" She reached across and lightly slapped his shoulder. "Right, you've done it now... I'm turning the key and starting this beast!" The engine fired as she spoke. She turned to look at him. "Oh, Dante... this is mine! My first ever car! Well, it's more like a truck, really... But it's still my first ever car! I love you so much! Thank you!" She leaned across to kiss his cheek and then put the Hummer into reverse. Lari steered around the Viper and navigated the turning circle to drive back towards the road.

"Where are we going, beautiful?" Dante asked her, looking pleased at her obvious happiness.

"You can wait and see now," she told him. "My turn to surprize you."

TWELVE

Lari drove through Roswell and south onto Route 285S. Turning left onto US380E, she drove into Texas.

"Are you going to tell me where we're going yet?" Dante asked as she stayed silent. He tried to read her mind without success. "Shielding your thoughts too... Meanie."

"Nope. I told you. You have to wait and see."

"Well, I know we're in Texas. Are we staying in Texas or going somewhere else? You can tell me that much, surely." Dante tried a slightly different question.

"Yeah, we're in Texas. Didn't you see that road sign? The one that said 'Don't mess with Texas'." She grinned at him. "Well, I have one to add to that. Don't mess with Lari." She laughed. "I'm not telling you where we're going until we get there, so be patient!"

Around a hundred miles along the road, she turned into Route 385S. Seeing the fuel gauge dropping lower, Larissa pulled into the first gas station she saw. "Ok, Mr Money, feed my hungry SUV please!" she told him. Dante obligingly got out, pumped the gas and paid for it.

"Still not going to tell me where we're going?" he asked as he jumped back into the Hummer.

"Nope," she laughed, pulling out of the gas station and driving for just over another hundred miles. Even though she'd logged hundreds of miles learning to drive, this was her first long-distance drive and she was surprised to discover that it didn't tire her.

"When I said, did you want to go for a drive, I didn't mean a cross-country tour. I didn't pack a bag," Dante joked as it became obvious they were driving further.

"Yeah... Y'know, I thought long-distance driving was supposed to be tiring but I guess it's not."

"Not for us, baby. We just don't get tired for any reason."

Nearly six hours after she left home, she parked the Hummer on the side of the road.

"Can I have my camera, Dante?" He handed it to her and she hopped out of the vehicle.

"You brought us to the Pecos oil fields?" he asked as he joined her on the roadside.

"Yeah," she answered as she started taking photos. "When you first started teaching me to drive, I looked up where it was and decided it would be one of the first places I drove myself to. It's amazing. I'd heard about it... The largest oil field or something, isn't it? I've never seen anything like it and I wanted to see it and it really is amazing to look at."

"Y'know it's probably good that we don't have to breathe coz I think the smell would be pretty intense." Dante frowned slightly as he sniffed the air. "Oh God! It is intense!"

Lari laughed. "Why did you sniff when you said it was good we don't breathe? That was stupid, but funny."

"Because I am stupid but funny," he laughed with her. "Not stupid enough to breathe again, though. That's a smell I'm going to remember for a while." He looked around at the hundreds of wells on the horizon. "Kind of noisy too, isn't it?"

"Yeah... Not the tourist trip you thought I was going to take you on, hey?" she asked as she took more photos, this time making sure he was in the pictures too.

"No baby, I would never have guessed we were coming here. Here, give me the camera," he said. She handed it to him. "Stand over there." She crossed the road to where he'd directed.

"Here, Dante?" she asked.

"Perfect." He snapped a few photos, zooming in on the last two. "My beloved against a background of oil wells..." She danced around a little as he switched the camera into video mode and captured her antics. "You know baby, in all the years I've been coming to America, I don't think I've ever thought to visit here."

"Really? So you haven't been here before?"

"Well, I think I may have driven through or past, but no, I've never stopped and looked around."

"Good. I brought you somewhere new then. New car, new driver, new place to visit. Lotsa new things in one go."

He stopped taking photos and joined her, lifting her off the ground and swinging her around. "I love you, beautiful. Everything feels new with you."

She kissed him. "I love you too. Now put me down coz we're outta here. I think we've seen all there is to see."

"Where are we off to now then?"

"The Alamo."

He looked at her. "You're not kidding, are you?"

"Hey, you tell me all the time that we don't need sleep and why do we need to bring a change of clothes or anything with us? We're not travelling with any humans who are going to ask questions. Or staying anywhere with them. So,

44

let's be random and see some things!"

He laughed. "You make a very good point. Maybe I've just been mixing in the human world so long I just think a little bit human." He paused. "But you're right. We don't need sleep. We're not travelling with humans. We don't need the human things like a change of clothes. So, let's go. To the Alamo, beautiful girl." He paused again, grinning. "You do know how far it is, right?"

"Nah. Haven't got a clue. All I know is it's in Texas and we're in Texas. It's an adventure."

He laughed. "We can stop at the next gas station or truckstop and buy a map... or I can wait till you're hopelessly lost and get a map to help you find it then."

"Let's get lost first. It's more of an adventure and it's not like we have to be anywhere by any special time."

"Lost it is, then. Drive, my baby." They both jumped back into the Hummer and Larissa drove off in the direction the SUV was facing.

"Just one thing, Dante... I am sort of going in the right direction, aren't I?"

"Yeah, I think so. But if you leave Texas, I think you'll have made a wrong turn."

"Nope, no leaving Texas until we find the Alamo." She grinned and put her foot down, glancing across to the west. "Look at the sunset over there! Isn't it beautiful?"

Dante looked west. "Very beautiful. And you're actually driving faster than I think I've ever experienced with you!"

"Ooooh, y'know, a thumping is coming your way if you keep being so cheeky!" she laughed. "Seriously, I think I like this vehicle. I feel safe in it. Maybe coz it's so big. So I think you can expect faster travel from me nowadays."

"Good. I like fast."

THIRTEEN

It should only have been another six hours to the Alamo, but Lari saw a sign to a town named Marathon and just had to detour through it. Then she saw another sign and took off in a new direction. Seeing another sign, she changed direction again, and finally back on the I-10, she saw a sign for a town named Iraan and headed off in that direction till she found that town. Eventually Dante decided she was going to zig-zag the entire way to the Alamo and let it happen without reminding her that she was heading the wrong way again.

Each time the Hummer needed fuel, Larissa told Dante to fill it up for her and he obligingly did, telling her on the last occasion, "You will have to learn to do this yourself, you know. What happens if I'm not with you and you need fuel?"

"Well, I'd be in serious trouble then coz how would I pay for it, either? You have all the money," she retorted.

"Ah, yes... the money." He got out, pumped the gas and paid for it without saying more until he got back into the Hummer. "Before you drive off baby, I have something for you."

"Oooh, what? Is it another present?" Lari asked eagerly.

"Kind of." He reached into his wallet and removed a credit card. "This is yours," he told her as he handed it over.

Lari smiled and took it from him. "A credit card? Ooooh, baby... I can shop!"

Dante laughed. "As much as you want."

"Yeah, I wouldn't say that Dante... you've no idea how much I can shop!" She pocketed the credit card and leaned across to plant a kiss on his lips. "Thank you, honey."

"No problems, beautiful. I should've given you a card earlier. I just forgot about it."

"I haven't needed it so it doesn't matter, but it will be useful now I have my own car." She fired up the engine and drove off. "And I won't go silly buying things. I'm just teasing you about that."

They pulled over in a lay-by around midnight and fed from sleeping occupants in the few RVs parked in darkness. Jumping back into the Hummer a short while later, Larissa decided it was time to find out where they were. "So, Dante, what road am I on now?"

"The I-10. The one you should be on if we're ever going to get to San Antonio."

"Why do we want to go to San Antonio?"

"Because that's where the Alamo is."

"Oh, is it? So that's where I'm supposed to be going?"

Dante laughed, "Well, if you still want to go the Alamo, then, yes."

"Oh yeah, of course I do! There's some pretty cool names for towns here, though. I can't help it if I'm curious and want to see those towns!" She smiled at Dante. "How much longer for us to get there?"

"Well... Let's see... we should've been there by now but we've taken the very scenic route and now we're further away than we started... so... I think we're probably just over six hours away."

"No, really?" Lari looked disbelieving. "How big is Texas?"

"It's big, but not that big." He shook his head. "You started out going in the right direction but then you went in so many different directions chasing towns with names that caught your attention that we're now west of Fort Stockton and we started out about level with Fort Stockton. So, after all this driving, we're still about six hours from San Antonio."

"Wanna see how long we can stay six hours from there?" she asked him mischievously.

He shook his head, grinning. "Don't you dare... We could spend the rest of our lives in Texas, never leaving the highways... Never getting to the Alamo..."

"I should see how long we can stay this far away... It could be fun..." She laughed. "Don't look so worried, I won't... But maybe one day..."

"Y'know, baby, I think I've created a monster, teaching you to drive... You're never gonna stop driving now, are you?" He grinned to let her know he wasn't serious.

"Monster? You wanna call me a monster? Oooooh, I'll give you monster... you just wait!"

"Oh no, what are you going to do to me? Am I gonna get thumped again?"

"Nah, you like that too much... I'll have to think about this... Monster! Ha!"

"Still haven't said you'll ever stop driving, I notice..."

"Yeah... Maybe that'll be your punishment... I'm gonna drive forever and you're stuck in the passenger seat beside me..." She grinned at him.

"The eternal passenger, that's me..."

"Never getting to the Alamo!" she laughed.

Dante joined in the laughter. "Oh baby, it's so much fun travelling with you. I know I've seen lots of these places before but I don't think I ever noticed them. And even if it takes us another day to get to the Alamo, this is a great trip."

"Thanks, Dante." Larissa smiled at him and reached across to brush his cheek gently with her fingertips. "I'm having so much fun, too." She looked at the road ahead, then back to him. "Alamo it is... no more detours. Let's be a couple of tourists."

"We'll probably be the first ones there," Dante told her.

"Ok, then maybe we can fit in another detour or two. Don't wanna get there too early, do we?"

"Nope, course not. Hey, can I pick the next detour?"

"Sure. Where do you want to go?"

"There's a town in Texas called Abilene and every time I've seen the sign, it's made me think of abalone so I'd like to make that one of our detours."

"Sure, let's go to Abalone!"

"Abilene."

"Nah, in honour of your first requested detour, we're renaming it Abalone. You better give me directions coz I have no idea where it is or how to get there."

"Ok, take this exit."

"Abalone, here we come!" she cheered as she took the turn-off.

FOURTEEN

Three days after they left their home in Roswell to take Lari's new SUV for a drive, they finally pulled in the driveway again.

"Home sweet home, Dante... see I didn't keep you on the road forever," she joked.

"It was a close call... there were times I thought you were going to," he joked back.

"I'm not physically tired but I think I am over the driving thing for a little while. You can drive us somewhere next time."

"What about surfing? My car doesn't cart boards."

"Then you can drive mine."

"Hmmmnnn, I like mine better."

"Don't care. Next trip's a surfing holiday and you can drive for at least some of it." She parked the Hummer behind Dante's Viper and jumped out. "You know what? I think I'm gonna pretend to be human and have a long, hot shower with lotsa perfumey stuff."

"Yeah, I like hot showers. Do they really feel much different now you're not human?"

"Lots. Why? Didn't you ever have a hot shower before you were a vampire?"

"Nope. We didn't have hot running water back then, so I've only ever experienced hot showers as a vamp." Dante unlocked the front door and they headed up the stairs.

"Wow, I never realized that." She paused and thought about what she said next. "Ok, so they don't feel the same but the water warms my skin up if it's really hot but I don't feel warmer... Does that make sense to you? I mean, I don't feel hot or cold anymore... I know what you meant when you tried to explain to me how you didn't feel cold in the cold weather we had when you and I first met."

"Yeah, I think I understand what you're saying. Do the showers feel as good as they used to... before... when you were human?"

"I think so... but different. I always loved a hot shower, y'know... It was kinda a fix-everything... Could be relaxing or refreshing or just a shower. That's the same. I still like to relax in the shower and I can breathe and smell all the perfumey things if I want to."

They reached the upstairs bathroom and stopped outside the door. "Good. So, do you want to shower by yourself or can I join you?" Dante asked with a mischievous smile.

"I've never shared a shower before... so... yup, you can join me!" she laughed. "It's gonna be girlie and perfumey, though... Can you handle that?"

"Haha, not a problem... If it gets too much, I just won't breathe, and I've never showered with anyone either. It'll be a first for both of us," he told her.

"Not having to breathe can be such an awesome thing, hey?" she asked him with a smile. "Though some funny people inhale even after they say how good it is that they don't have to breathe," she reminded him.

"Yeah, I wanted to know what it was like, okay... And perfumey showers aren't gonna smell anything like the Pecos oilfields... or at least, I hope they don't!" he retorted with a laugh.

Lari stepped into the bathroom while Dante walked down the hall to the linen press. She ran the hot water till the room started to steam up, lighting some scented candles while she waited for the water to get hot enough for her liking. Dante found some towels in the hall closet and brought them in, finding her already stripped naked and about to get under the water.

"You're not slow, are you?" he asked, dropping the towels on the bench next to the vanity and removing his own clothes. He joined her in the shower. "Shall I wash your back?" he asked.

She turned away from him. "There you are... my back. Is that what you wanted?"

He smiled and shook his head. "So, we're playing games, are we?" He reached for the soap and started lathering her back. "Fine. Your back it is." He grinned at the back of her head, "What's your next move then?"

"Oh, this will do for now," she smiled. "You might wanna try washing my front too, though..." she added.

"Mmmmnnn..." She felt him kissing the back of her neck as his soapy hands slipped round to caress her breasts. "Like this?" he asked huskily.

"Yeah, keep going... I like this..." she answered, leaning back into him, her eyes closing. Her own hands reached behind to clasp his hips and draw him closer to her.

She felt the excitement building as they rocked together, their soapy hands sliding across each other's bodies. Suddenly he spun her round and pressed her against the tiles, his lips against hers, their tongues dancing together. She climbed onto him as he entered her and thrust her against the wall, the hot water streaming down over them both and finally, she cried out in ecstasy as they slid into a heap at the base of the shower.

"Oh, I liked that, Dante," she whispered huskily, her eyes staring intently into his.

"Me too," he replied, beginning to move.

"No, don't move. Stay where you are," she told him. "Just for now. I want to stay like this for now... let the pleasure linger a bit."

"Okay." He remained still and kissed her gently.

FIFTEEN

A week after their mini-road trip through Texas, Lari raised the subject of a surfing holiday again. "So, Dante, where in California will we go surfing?"

"I know of a place called Mavericks," he answered. "Google it. Tell me if you like the sound of it. It is supposed to be a pretty dangerous beach but since we're not human, that's not really an issue for us."

"Mavericks? Cool name for a beach... Are there others?"

"I don't know."

"Okay, give me a minute." She ran upstairs and a few minutes later, returned with her macbook, sitting on the couch and opening the computer. "So, what should I Google?"

Dante laughed. "Just type Mavericks, maybe?"

"Ok... Mavericks..." She opened the browser, typed into the search bar and waited for the page to load. "Oh, wow... Dante, come here. I don't think all of these are for the beach," she told him, laughing. "Look at the pictures of those waves! Tell me what to click on."

He got up and joined her on the couch. "Try that one." He pointed at a link to the surf contest.

"Okay," she said as she clicked and waited for the page to load. "The Wave... I'm checking that one out," she told him as she selected the link.

"Good description."

"Yeah, I like this site." She studied the information. "It says the surfing is good from November to March... That's perfect since we wanna go surfing now." She continued to read. "So, we're definitely going here... I really like the sound of it and those pictures were fantastic. Are we going to go anywhere else too?"

"Where would you like to go?"

She kept studying the site, checking out the other links. "I don't know. Are there other beaches to surf at? Or I suppose we could just road-trip our way there and do some sight-seeing for other things."

"We could go via San Diego and check out the zoo. It's supposed to be pretty good."

"That'd be good. Where else?" She returned to the search page and scanned the list of links, selecting the link to images of Mavericks. "And how long can we go for?"

"We can go for as long as you want. As to where else, that's up to you too. Would you like to make it a round trip and return via Lake Tahoe? That's a beautiful part of the country."

"Great! That sounds brilliant Dante! Hey, Lake Tahoe is where Meg Ryan's character rides that bike with her eyes shut in City of Angels, right?" She looked up from the computer. "I am right, aren't I? It is Lake Tahoe, isn't it?" she added.

He laughed, "I don't know. I haven't seen the movie but if it's set in Lake Tahoe, we can find it and drive that stretch of road."

"Cool. You haven't seen it? Oh, you have to see the movie, too... I love that movie." She paused to look at the screen again, typing and clicking, before looking back at him, "You do know I'm not doing all the driving, right?"

Dante laughed again. "Yeah, I remember you telling me that when we got back from the trip to Texas."

"Yeah, I think I'll definitely make you drive that part of the trip. Those roads looked windy and mountainy."

"Is mountainy even a word?" he laughed.

Lari stopped hunching over the computer, stretched and laughed. "Yeah, I just invented it."

"Okay, then I'll drive the mountainy bit for you," he chuckled.

"So, we're going to San Diego and Mavericks and Lake Tahoe... Anywhere else?"

He shrugged. "I don't know. Anywhere you particularly want to go? Or we can wing it if you like..."

"I can't think of anywhere right now, but I might change my mind. And winging it is like the random exploring we did in Texas, right?"

"Yeah, that was winging it."

"Then we can do that. I'd like to go surfing this week so we can take off soon, can't we? I really miss it and you promised that we could once I had my Hummer."

"And we can. If you want to go this week, then we will."

"Wicked. Are we going to pretend to be human and stay in motels and things or are we just going to surf and drive and sightsee and drive," she asked.

"I think since we'll probably hang around the beach a while, and possibly other places, we should probably pretend to be human and try to blend in, at least some of the time."

"Okay. We should pack clothes and things to take with us then." Lari frowned and sighed. "Dante, one other thing..."

"Yes?"

"It's nothing to do with the trip or surfing... well, not directly..." She sighed again. "I still need to feed every day and it's more than a month since I became a vampire. Actually, it's more than two months now, nearly three. How long before that changes?"

"I don't know, baby. You don't feed quite as much... I mean, when you were first made, you fed more than once a day or you fed fully from several people so you could last the day, so it has lessened because it really is only once a day now that you need to feed and you only feed from one person or you take small amounts from several, which is the same as feeding properly from one. How long since you felt that desperate hunger?"

"Not for ages... I'd forgotten that I used to feel like that, even feeding every day..."

"See, it is lessening."

"Yeah, I guess so... I just wish I only needed to feed every few days like you."

"Baby, compared to you, I'm ancient!" He put his arm around her and hugged. "Don't forget, I'm over a hundred years old as a vampire and you're not even three months."

She laughed. "I always forget you're so old."

"Thanks, beautiful. I'm not sure how to take that." He grinned at her. "Feel better?"

"Yeah, I do. Thanks, Dante." She rested her head on his shoulder. "C'mon, let's plan this trip."

SIXTEEN

"Dante! Where are you?" Lari called from upstairs. "I don't know what you want me to pack for you." She threw more clothes into the duffel bag she'd bought for herself a few days ago. "Oh, I know you can hear me," she muttered.

"Lari, it's okay. I'll be there soon," she heard his voice in her head.

"Fine," she muttered. "Well, then I'm just gonna pack my own stuff and you can figure out what you want," she told the empty room, knowing he could hear her wherever he was.

She removed the last two things she'd hurled into her bag and replaced them with a couple of swimsuits and another pair of jeans. "Ohhhh, I don't know what to take," she groaned to herself.

"Dante, do I need to pack towels or stuff like that?" she called to him.

"No," he answered in her head again.

"Where are you? Why are you in my head and not talking out loud?"

"I'm outside, making sure the Hummer's ready for the trip."

"Oh, okay then." She returned to packing her bag. "There, that's it," she told herself, looking at the contents. "If I forgot anything, too bad. I'm over this packing." She zipped up her duffel and frowned as she looked at the empty duffel she'd bought for him when she bought hers. Suddenly she sensed him right behind her and spun around. "There you are. About time. I'm packed."

"You could've just thrown a bunch of jeans and tops in for me," he told her as he proceeded to do just that.

"What are you going to wear surfing?"

"Boardshorts and T-shirts?" he asked, tossing some into his bag.

"Okay," she answered. "You did say it would be good for us to blend in. Will that blend in?"

"Maybe." He studied the contents of his bag. "That'll do, anyway." He smiled at her as he zipped his duffel closed. "I packed wetsuits and our boards into the Hummer already."

"Oh, okay. Thanks." She hoisted her duffel. "Did the boards fit inside?"

"Don't know. I never thought to try. They're actually on the roof. I fitted some racks for them."

"Oh, cool. So, are we ready now?"

"Yeah, hop in the Hummer and I'll lock up and join you."

"So, who's driving first?"

"You are. Your Hummer, so you can do the first leg of our journey."

"Alright... but you are going to drive too, y'know."

"I'm sure you'll make it happen," he laughed. "Go on, get in while I lock up."

Lari raced out of the room and downstairs, tossing her bag into the back of the Hummer and getting behind the wheel. A few minutes later, Dante appeared and tossed his bag in the back next to hers, joining her in the passenger seat.

"So where's the Viper?" she asked, noticing that it wasn't anywhere in sight.

"Parked in the garage down the back."

"Oh, wow. That's a garage? I never realized."

"You're so observant sometimes," he teased her.

Ignoring the jibe, she asked, "Ready to go?"

"Yup," he answered. "Do you need directions?"

"Yeah, I think so."

"Okay, turn left at our gate and then when you reach the highway, turn right."

"How far do I go along the highway?"

"A long way... It sort of merges with other major routes so just keep following the Route 70 west signs. I'll let you know before you need to turn anywhere." He paused. "You have noticed the sat-nav I installed, haven't you?"

"Is that what that is?" she asked. "You can operate it. I'll crash if I try to do that and drive."

"Ok, beautiful."

"So, do you actually know where we need to go or are you going to map it on the new sat-nav thingie?" she asked, suspicious of his vague directions and reference to the sat-nav.

He grinned. "I can get us to San Diego but then I need to map it. I've heard of Mavericks but I've never been there. We're about thirteen hours from San Diego, so do you want to drive straight there or see things on the way?"

"You could've looked it up last night or something," she told him.

"Was busy," he answered, grinning at her. "You remember, don't you? You were there."

She laughed. "That didn't take all night... Not the way I remember, anyway."

Lari stopped at the gate, checking for traffic before turning left onto the road. "Which way do I turn when I get to Route 70 again?" she asked him.

"Right," he reminded her. Dante removed the sat-nav unit from its mount, turning it on and tapping the touch screen. He stared at it for a few minutes, then turned it off and replaced it in its mount. "Well, that's a long drive we've got ahead of us," he told her. "It's around thirteen hours to San Diego and according to this it's around another eight hours to Mavericks."

"Lucky we don't need sleep and don't get tired then, isn't it?" She grinned as she made the right turn onto Route 70. "You'll be driving for some of it, y'know."

"So you keep reminding me. You didn't answer me before. Do you want to stop and look around at places on the way or just go straight there?"

"Looking around sounds good. It's not like we have a time limit or anything, is it?" He shook his head. "Anywhere you suggest?"

"There's probably lots of places. I've got to be honest, sweetie, I've never done a road trip like this before."

"Well, this will be something new for both of us then."

"Yeah... Don't blame me if we get lost on the way, though," he told her.

"Oh, of course I will! But I'll still love you," she giggled. "Just remember to give me plenty of warning before I need to turn anywhere and I'll always forgive you if you get us lost."

He laughed. "I'll make sure to do that."

"You better," she warned him. "You know how I hate last minute instructions!"

"I know."

"Good, coz the first last minute direction you give me, I'm making you take over driving."

Dante laughed. "I'll be sure to tell you long before you need to know then. If I always give you plenty of notice, will that mean I never have to drive this?"

"No. Don't think you can get out of it like that coz you can't." She glanced across at him. "What's wrong with my Hummer, anyway?"

"Nothing except it's not a fast little sports car."

"Nah, it's a tough beast that can carry our boards so we can go surfing!" she laughed. "You are going to drive it so don't whinge."

"Meanie," he retorted, still laughing. "Turn right in a couple of miles but make sure you stay following the Route 70 west signs."

SEVENTEEN

About seven hours after they left home, they arrived in Tucson. It was just after three in the afternoon, at the beginning of the peak hour traffic. Lari was overwhelmed by the congestion and quickly found somewhere to pull over.

"You're driving now, Dante," she told him as she leaped out.

"Not a fan of the city traffic?" he laughed, getting out of the passenger side and into the driver seat. Lari hopped into the passenger side.

"Nope. Not at all. The traffic in San Diego will be even worse, won't it?" she asked him.

"Yeah, probably. Depends on what time of day or night we get there. It'll get worse here over the next few hours and then it'll get better again. Same thing will happen in San Diego."

"Then you'll drive there too," she informed him. Changing the subject, she asked, "Is there anything to sightsee here or do we keep going?"

"I don't know. Are you sick of the driving?" he asked.

"Actually, no, I'm not. But if there's something cool to see, since we're here, we could have a look around."

"Well, there's an observatory somewhere nearby that's supposed to be pretty good and since you like checking out towns with interesting names, there's a town called Tombstone," he said, starting the engine. "We might have to turn around to see them, though... Not too sure on my directions. I'd have to use the sat-nav to get to them." He paused to glance at her, "So, do we drive on or look around?"

"Let's check them out... Both of them."

"Okay, sounds good. Do you want to look them up on the sat-nav for me?"

"Sure." She reached for the sat-nav and removed it from its holder. "So, how do I use this?"

"Just turn it on and tap the information into it. You'll see. It's pretty straightforward."

"Okay." She turned it on. "Okay, so what do I type into this? Looks like I need to know the address of where I want to go."

"Hmmnn, that could be a problem. I don't know what the observatory is called. Or anything about Tombstone except its name."

"Is there some tourist place we could go to get that info?"

"Yeah, there probably is. Good idea, baby." He looked around. "Aha, that looks like a good direction to start." He pulled out into the traffic, turning at the next set of lights and pulling into a fast food restaurant carpark.

"What are we doing here, Dante?" Lari looked at him, astonished.

"Finding the tourist info place or the name of the observatory or how to get to Tombstone." He turned off the engine. "Come on, let's go ask some people where these places are."

They got out and walked into the restaurant, joining one of the queues for food.

"Look Dante, there's brochures over there... Looks like touristy stuff..." Larissa ran and grabbed a handful of them, returning to stand with him in the queue. Flicking through them, she told him, "Nothing on the observatory or Tombstone. Bummer."

They reached the counter. "Can I take your order?" asked the server.

"Ah, yes," answered Dante. "Can we get two large fries and a couple of regular cokes?"

"Two large fries and two regular cokes," repeated the server.

"Yes."

"Is that eat-in or takeaway?"

"Takeaway."

"That will be five dollars and thirty cents."

Dante handed over the money. "Ah, we're trying to find an observatory that's somewhere near here, but we don't know the name so we can't find it. You couldn't help us with that, could you?"

"That'd be Kitt Peak Observatory on the reservation."

"Kitt Peak. Thank you. It's on a reservation?"

"Yes, the Tohono O'odham Indian reservation. It's not too far from here. Take the I-19 south and then the exit to Highway 86. You'll go past Ryan Airfield and there'll be a turn-off to Kitt Peak. The observatory is at the summit of Kitt Peak. Are you going to one of the night programs?"

"Great, thanks. Uh, yes... one of the night programs. We want to go to Tombstone too. You couldn't point us in the right direction to get there, could you?"

"Are you going from here or from the reservation?"

"Ah, from the reservation."

"Well, you'd drive back towards here, get onto the I-10 east and take the Tombstone exit... That's AZ80."

"Thanks. You've been a great help."

"No problem." He handed them their food and drinks. "Enjoy your meal."

"Sure." Dante took the food and they walked out of the restaurant.

"And what are we doing with this?" Lari asked him quietly, nudging his hand that held the bag of food.

"We'll dump it in a bin somewhere. Come on. We've got directions to both places now, so let's start exploring."

EIGHTEEN

They reached the observatory in a short while and discovered that night programs were scheduled for that evening but they were supposed to be booked in advance. Not wanting to leave without doing the night observing program, they needed to compel the guides to believe they had already booked and the booking had just been lost. It worked, and very apologetic that they'd somehow been forgotten, the guides allowed them to join the group.

The light meal was easily avoided and Lari was thrilled to watch the sun set. They stayed for the full three and a half hours that the program lasted and Lari was bubbling with joy as they drove away, heading for Tombstone.

"Oh Dante! Weren't the stars magical? And the sunset was so romantic. That was the best place to visit. I'm so glad you suggested it."

"Yeah, it was good. Might have to go there again someday, if you like."

"Oh yes, Dante! Please! Next time we can do one of the daytime things or the overnight program." Almost With You by The Church started playing on the Hummer's stereo. "Oh, I love this song!" she exclaimed, turning the volume up and singing along. Dante grinned as he watched her. The song ended and she lowered the volume. "Since I met you, this is my favourite band now," she told him.

"Why?"

"There's this song of theirs, You Took, that I really love and when we first met, the words seemed really appropriate... and then I went home, thinking about you and the song came on my iPod... y'know... kinda like fate." She grinned shyly at him. "I'm telling you my secrets here."

He shook his head. "You still haven't told me why they're your favourite band now."

She rolled her eyes. "Coz, they just are."

He laughed. "Crazy beautiful. Those songs are older than you are."

Her eyes widened. "Don't care. They're great songs and that whole CD makes me think of you." Changing the subject, she asked him, "You'll tell me where and when to turn so we go to Tombstone, won't you? Or is it signposted?"

"Yeah, I'll tell you even if it's signed," he laughed. "Not going to sing some more?" he asked her.

"Nah, not until there's another song I can't resist."

"Get onto the I-10 east just up ahead." Dante flicked at the stereo controls, skipping through the songs until he reached The Killers performing Somebody Told Me. "Going to sing along with this one?" he asked.

"Hmnn... Well, I like it..." She hummed a bit. "Maybe I'll sing a bit," she told him as she turned onto the I-10 east. "Where to next?"

"There'll be an exit... AZ80... that's what that guy told us, wasn't it?"

"You're asking me?"

"Yeah, that was a waste of time, wasn't it..." he laughed as her eyes opened wide and she thumped his shoulder. "I'm sorry. You set yourself up for that."

"Ooooh! I'll get you now, you just wait..." she told him as she poked her tongue out at him and laughed.

"Cheeky," he grinned. "Oh look, AZ80... that's it. Take that exit."

"Where?" she asked him, unable to see any exit.

"Sorry, false alarm... but you did say you wanted plenty of notice."

"Yeah, there's a difference between lotsa notice and being a smartarse. You've crossed the line into smartarse territory. There'll be thumping if it continues," she retorted with a smile.

"Sorry, beautiful. I think we keep going down this road for a while yet. Should I find another song for you to sing along to?"

"Nah, I'm good just listening for now. The road's so empty. I thought there'd be more cars."

"Time of day, day we're travelling. It's not like we're the only vehicle on the road."

"True. But the traffic this afternoon was madness. Where did all those cars go?"

Dante laughed. "They went home."

"You're so funny. Haha." Larissa frowned as she glanced at the gauges on the dash. "We're gonna need fuel soon. How much further to Tombstone? Or somewhere we can get fuel. And on a more serious note... Dante, I'm getting kinda thirsty. Any chance of some people to drink from sometime soon-ish?"

"Well... not much chance of an invite into someone's house at this hour... and is better if they're sleeping anyway... Can you sense anyone about? Your senses will be a bit more alert than mine if you're thirsty."

"No. I can't sense anyone."

"Okay... just stay alert and hopefully we'll come across some sleepers... If we're lucky, the fuelstop will be deserted and camera-free and you can feed there. There's gotta be somewhere to get fuel soon."

They kept driving along the highway silently, listening to the stereo. Without warning, Larissa suddenly seemed more alert. She lowered her window and sniffed the air. "Dante... there's someone near here... Really near here coz I can smell the blood."

"It's probably a house. That won't do us any good. You can't get in without an invite."

"Are you sure it's a house? Where are any houses? I haven't seen any."

Suddenly the headlights lit up a hitchhiker on the side of the road a few hundred metres ahead of them, walking in the same direction as they were travelling, his thumb out, a big backpack strapped to his shoulders.

"Food, Dante! No house, just a pedestrian on the highway." She started slowing down, stopping just in front of him.

"Yes. An awake pedestrian. Be careful, Lari."

The hitchhiker reached the Hummer and jumped in the back, tossing his backpack onto the seat first. "Hey, thanks guys. I've walked a long way. Didn't think anyone was gonna stop. Name's Jeremy."

"I'm Dante and this is Larissa," Dante told him. "Do you want me to compel him for you, beautiful?" he asked Lari telepathically.

"Yes, please," she answered the same way. "I'm just looking for somewhere discreet to pull over."

"Hi Dante, Larissa. I'm heading to Houston. How far are you guys going?"

"Not to Houston." Dante turned to face Jeremy. "So, Jeremy, it's pretty comfortable in the back there?" He focused his attention on compelling Jeremy to his will.

"Uh, yeah. It's really good." Jeremy was staring back at Dante, unaware that he was falling under his spell.

"Great. You're falling asleep there."

"Yeah, I'm tired. Think I'm falling asleep. You don't mind, do you?" Jeremy yawned, blinking rapidly.

"Not at all. Sleep well."

"Yeah, think I will." Jeremy's eyes closed and a few minutes later he was softly snoring.

"There's a rest stop just ahead, beautiful. Did you see the sign?"

"Yeah." She pulled into the rest stop, parking well away from the only other vehicle there. "I'm really thirsty now. Should I get out and jump in the back or climb over the seat?"

"Play it safe. Climb over the seat." Dante looked at the other vehicle. "I can't tell if they're awake or asleep in that car."

"Okay." She wriggled her way into the back seat and started drinking from Jeremy, whispering to him the familiar story that she was just a dream. A short while later she was done and the other vehicle had driven away. "So, we're alone now. Guess they were awake." She exited from the back seat using the door this time and hopped back into the driver's seat. "I feel much better now. What are we going to do with him?"

"Well, he's still sleeping... and when he wakes, he'll think it was a dream... so how about we wake him when we stop for fuel and tell him that's it for us and we're turning off so he's out."

"Okay." She started the Hummer and drove back onto the I-10. Twenty-five minutes later she saw the AZ80 exit. "Damn... Dante... we have to wake him here." She brought the truck to a stop just before the exit.

Dante turned and leaned over the back. "Jeremy... hey, Jeremy! Time to wake up." He reached over and gave his shoulders a light shake. "Jeremy, you gotta wake up."

Jeremy groaned and his eyes blinked open. "Hey... did I fall asleep?"

"Yeah, you've been out. Said you were tired and fell asleep pretty much straight away."

"Damn weird dreams..." He rubbed his eyes. "Sorry, man. I've been lousy company."

"It's okay. Look, we've got to let you out here. We're taking this exit so it's as far as we can take you."

"Oh, sure... Thanks for the ride. Saved me a few miles of walking. Must've needed sleep too." He grabbed his backpack and got out of the Hummer. "Safe travels. Bye," he told them as he shut the door and waved.

"Bye Jeremy. Safe travels." Dante called out the window as Lari drove off, heading for the exit.

NINETEEN

As they reached Benson, they saw the sign for a gas station. "Fuel, Dante," Lari told him. "Y'know, I'm still a bit thirsty... I guess I was a bit quick to stop drinking from that guy. What do u think's my chance of another meal?"

"You might be lucky. Be careful, though... There's usually cameras in these places and they're pretty well lit up."

She pulled up to the pump, spying a middle-aged woman walking into the Ladies toilets. "Ooooh, I think I have the answer... Put fuel in the beast. I need a trip to the Ladies..." They both jumped out, Dante pumping gas while Lari disappeared into the toilets.

By the time he'd finished and paid for the fuel, Lari walked out from the toilets, holding the woman's elbow. Seeing Dante looking in their direction, she waved him over. "Dante! Can you come over here please?"

Dante joined them by the door to the ladies. "Is everything all right?" he asked.

"Yes. This is Eleanor. She was in the toilets and she fainted. She's feeling a bit unsteady."

Dante took the woman's other elbow. "Come, let's get you a hot tea. That'll make you feel better," he told her.

"Oh, no need. I don't know what happened. I remember washing my hands and next thing your wife was leaning over me, helping me up from the floor."

"Are you sure?" he asked, continuing to lead her away from the toilets.

"Yes, yes... I feel fine now, really. That's my car over there." She gently removed her arm from Dante's hold and pointed at a blue sedan. "I think I'll head home. It's not far. I'll be fine." She turned to smile at Lari who had also released her grip. "Thank you for your help, dear. Sorry if I gave you a fright."

"No problem," Lari answered her. "You're sure you're okay now?"

"Yes, yes. I don't know what came over me. I really think I'll just go straight home. I'm probably overtired. It is late."

"Okay, you take care, Eleanor." Larissa waved to her as the woman walked to her car and got in.

"Clever girl," Dante whispered to Lari, smiling and waving at Eleanor driving off.

"Was quick thinking, wasn't it? And really easy. I'm getting much better at compelling people, y'know."

They got back into the Hummer and continued the journey to Tombstone.

"So, what did you actually tell her?" Dante asked as they sped along in the darkness.

"Just that she'd fainted and she couldn't remember anything. It worked. First I told her she was going to sleep so I could drink, but I didn't tell her I was going to drink... And then after, I said you'll wake up in a minute and you won't remember anything that happened after you washed your hands. And then when she did wake up, I told her she'd fainted and she believed me."

"Going into the toilets was a great idea. I've never thought of that before but there's not usually cameras there."

"No, and it's easy enough to get some privacy too. I drank from her in a cubicle in case someone else came in and then I put her on the floor in front of the basin before I woke her up."

"Like I said, clever thinking."

"So, how much further is Tombstone?"

"Not much further now. Do you want to look around a bit once we arrive or are we going to return to aiming for San Diego zoo as soon as we get there?"

"Wait and see." She frowned as she drove along the dark highway. "What time is it, Dante? Y'know I just realized I've lost all sense of time... When we first met it always amazed me how good you were at knowing the time and now, it amazes me even more, coz I really just have no idea of the time."

"I actually don't know, beautiful, and I'm not wearing a watch. I usually only wear them when I have flights to catch at airports." He reached into the glovebox and pulled out his phone. "This has the time," he told her. "Give me a minute. It's not on." He turned it on and waited for the screen to load. "It's nearly 11pm." He switched it off and returned it to the glovebox.

"I still don't get it. How come you were so good at knowing what the time was back then, but not so much now?"

"I know I told you it was because I came from a different time and stuff, but it's not. It was because I needed to be aware of the time. I was going to uni and doing other things like dating you, and I couldn't just turn up anytime I felt like it. I had to be there when I was supposed to. Now you and I are free of those restraints. We can do anything and go anywhere anytime we like, so now I'm not as aware of what the time is."

"But I never saw you wearing a watch except that time when we were at the airport."

"Yeah, I don't really wear a watch that often, but there were always clocks around and I'd check them... and I suppose a part of that thing about coming from a different time was maybe true because I can tell roughly what the time is by how far the sun is along the horizon, especially if I've checked a clock not long before."

"Okay. How come you didn't explain that to me before?"

"I don't know. I guess I liked being a bit mysterious for you."

She glanced at him, then returned to watching the road, grinning, and shook her head. "What, being a vampire wasn't mystery enough?"

"Yeah, well, I probably didn't think it through," he grinned back at her.

"Nah, not at all," she laughed.

TWENTY

Two days later they were back on the I-10 heading for San Diego again. After spending some time looking around Tombstone, Lari had stumbled across a sign for a town named Apache and detoured through there so now they were even further east of Tucson.

Dante had his Macbook open on his lap and was uploading all the photographs and videos that Lari had taken in Tombstone and Apache.

"You take an extravagant amount of pictures, beautiful. By the time we get to Mavericks I'll have a computer full of pictures and videos and no room for anything else."

"Are you complaining about how long it takes to upload coz if you want, you can take over the driving and I'll do that. And you should be uploading them to my macbook, not yours."

"Yeah, I probably should be. We can transfer them later." He grinned at her. "Actually, we'll be going through Tucson again soon, so you can stop and I'll take over if you like since I bet you'll make me drive through there again anyway."

"Oh, yes, that traffic. I don't want to drive in that." She quickly slowed down and pulled over on the side of the highway. Leaving the engine running, she jumped out and went round the passenger side, opening the door. "C'mon. Out. You're driving now. I'll do that."

Dante placed the computer on the seat and hopped out. Lari quickly jumped in, lifting the Macbook onto her lap and continuing uploading the photos and videos. Dante got into the driver's seat and they started moving again.

"So, we're not stopping in Tucson this time are we?" he asked her.

"Nah, we've done that... although I loved that observatory... but no, we can do that again another time and I really do wanna surf sometime soon. The sightseeing's good, but y'know this is supposed to be a surfing trip and none of that's happened yet."

"Okay, so we'll go straight through Tucson then."

"Do we just stay on this I-10 forever?"

Dante laughed. "No. What makes you say that?"

"Well, when we cruised around Texas... when I got this... it seemed like we always ended up back on the I-10... and we're on the I-10 again, just going in a different direction."

"Well, soon we'll be on the I-8."

"'Kay." She looked thoughtful, staring out at the scenery. "But I bet we end up back on the I-10 again, though."

Dante laughed. "Yeah, maybe. For a bit. But maybe not... I think it's the I-5 we get on to after the I-8... that should take us to San Diego and Maverick's, I think... and we'll be a long way from the I-10 when we head for Lake Tahoe."
"If you say so."
"What have you got against the I-10?"
"Nothing. I'd just like to check out a different road."
Dante laughed. "I'm sure you'll see plenty of different roads on this trip."
She pulled a face at him, and then her eyes widened. "Oh, Dante... I didn't think about it before coz I was sidetracked... y'know, sightseeing and stuff... but I'm gonna be thirsty in a few hours. And you haven't fed in a few days. How are you going?"
"Yeah, I could handle feeding tonight, too. I like that toilet thing you did back in Benson."
"Toilet thing?"
"Yes... Feeding from that woman in the toilets at that fuel stop."
"Oh, that. Yeah, that was a good idea I had. So, shall we do that tonight?"
"Yeah. This thing just sucks down the gasoline so I think you should feed from one fuel stop and I'll feed from another."
"'Kay. Sounds good to me."
"What time is it?"
Lari frowned at the computer screen. "Says it's 4:55pm."
"Okay, so we want to feed after dark I think... so we'll probably stop in three to four hours time to feed."
"I'm good with that."
"Then that's the plan. Are you going to take over the driving after we get through Tucson?"
"Nah... You can feed first and I'll take over again after we stop for fuel and you feed. I think I'm a little bit bored of driving."
"You can video while we drive if you like."
"Hey, I can! Great idea, Dante. All the video's uploaded now, so I can unplug it." She removed the video cable, closing the Macbook and putting it away in its case. She reached over the back and gently dropped it onto the seat. Picking up the video camera from the floor where it had fallen, she started fiddling with the controls. "There... say cheese!" She pointed the camera at Dante who obligingly smiled. "Thank you," she smiled and winked at him as she swung the camera around to take in the view through the windscreen.
They slowed as the traffic increased and Lari continued filming. "Welcome to the Tucson traffic..." she announced as they slowed to a crawl. She panned the camera around to take in the congestion. "And this is why I'm not

driving," she added. She filmed for a short while longer and then turned off the camera, placing it on her lap. "So do you know where the next fuel stop is? I mean, are there going to be lotsa places we can stop or will we have to get off the interstate and go looking to find them?"

"Not sure... Hopefully there's a few near the interstate around the time we start looking for somewhere to stop but if not, I'm sure we'll find something not too far out of our way."

"'Kay..." she sounded doubtful.

"What's up? You sound..." he glanced across at her, frowning.

"It's okay... I'm just wondering if we'll ever get anywhere to surf." She smiled at him. "I'm just being moody. I know we'll get there and the sightseeing is good, Dante." She giggled, "Hey, did you notice? I'm learning to call it an interstate instead of a highway."

He grinned back at her, "Yes, you are."

The traffic started to clear and they picked up speed as they made their way out of Tucson and continued driving towards the I-8 and San Diego.

TWENTY-ONE

About four hours later they pulled into a fuel station near Yuma. Dante got out and filled the Hummer while his eyes scanned for a suitable target. Lari jumped out when he was done, responding to his silent request for her to go pay for the fuel.

While she was doing that, he cleaned the windscreen and checked the oil and coolant in the vehicle. When he saw her exit the doorway of the building, he jumped back into the Hummer and drove it to the nearby parking bay.

"Well, Dante?" she asked him. "You going to the toilet now and I'll take over driving when you get back?"

"Yeah... back in a few minutes," he told her, tossing her the keys. He casually disappeared into the Men's toilets, following a young man. A short while later, he returned alone. Jumping into the passenger seat, he turned to Lari, "Okay, let's go."

Her eyes grew wide as she started the engine. "Uh, what happened to the guy... or don't I want to know?" she asked as she reversed out.

"Nothing, really," he told her. "I fed from him and left him sitting in a cubicle passed out."

"Oh, okay... How long do you think he'll stay that way for?"

"He should be coming to now. I told him he'd sleep for five minutes. I thought about how you made up that story for that woman so I decided to do that too. You've taught me something, beautiful. All these years, I've never thought to do anything like this." He leaned across to kiss her cheek. "So, I told him that he'd felt off-colour when he went into the toilet and he'd gone into a cubicle and that was all he was going to remember when he came around."

"That's a good one. I'll have to think of my story now... I was just going to do what I did last time but now I think I should maybe come up with something better."

"It worked pretty good. You could do it again if you wanted."

"Yeah, but..." she grinned at him. "I feel challenged."

He laughed. "You feel challenged? But you taught me this."

"Yeah, but you kinda improved on it." She kept driving down the dark road. Headlights loomed off to the side. "What's that, Dante?" she asked, puzzled.

He looked across to where she could see the lights. "Oh, I think that's the Mexican highway. I don't know what it's called. The Mexican border's just over there somewhere."

"Oh, cool. I didn't know we were that close to Mexico."

"Yeah, right next to it."

The headlights were joined by more headlights and the flashing red and blue lights of official vehicles. "Looks like something interesting going on over there," she told him. A helicopter swept overhead, it's searchlight illuminating the area. "Oooh, look, they've got him!" she exclaimed as all the vehicles seemed to stop. "What do you think he did?"

"I have no idea. Could be anything. We're not going for a look, either."

She glanced over at Dante. "I wasn't going to suggest that, Dante. It's just the most interesting thing happening out here right now..." Her eyes returned to the road. "Shit!" she yelled, hitting the brakes as a body thumped loudly over the hood of the Hummer and the vehicle skidded along the road.

Dante leaped out as she came to a stop, the vehicle at an angle, facing the wrong way. "Stay there, Lari. Can you sense that?"

"Yes," she answered him.

"Lock the doors."

"Dante," she began.

"Lock the doors." He slammed the door shut and moved to stand in front of the Hummer, examining the hood. "Where are you and who are you?" he asked, staring along the dark road they'd just travelled. He sniffed the air. "There's two of you. Show yourselves now."

Lari stared wildly through the windscreen, her fear visible on her face. "Dante," she began again, not loud enough to be heard outside the vehicle, but knowing he could hear her.

"It's all right, beautiful, just stay there with the doors locked." He sniffed the air again. "We're not going anywhere until I know who you are and where you are, so show yourselves now."

One of the dark shadows on the side of the road moved, standing slowly and carefully. A second later, another smaller shadow separated itself from the darkness and stood next to the first. The two shadows stepped into the light from the Hummer's headlights.

The frenzy of action happening on the Mexican side of the border had increased. Most of the vehicles were stationary, but some were on the move again and the helicopter was now circling the area with spotlights searching.

The strangers glanced back at the Mexican border, at each other, and then looking straight at Dante, the man spoke in a thickly accented voice. "Help us get out of here or we'll all be discovered by them." He tilted his head in the direction of Mexico.

Dante looked at them cautiously. The man was almost the same height as him but stockier, and his female companion was a little taller than Lari and more curvaceous. They both had pale olive skin and blue eyes. He had light brown micro-braids falling to his mid-back, studded with beads, while her hair was waist-length, jet black and as full of curls as Lari's. Both were dressed in faded denim jeans and tight-fitting T-shirts. Their feet were bare. Sighing, Dante spoke, "You have a point. Tell me your names."

"I'm Slam and this is Jaz." Taking hold of Jaz's hand, he cautiously walked towards Dante. "We really should get out of here."

"Fine. You get in the back with me, Slam, and Jaz can get in the front with Lari. But as soon as we're on the move, I want more than just your names."

"Done. Let's go." Slam and Jaz picked up the pace and made for the Hummer. Lari unlocked the rear door behind her and then the passenger front door. Quickly, they all leapt in.

"Turn the beast around and let's go, Lari," Dante told her as he sat behind her and pulled the door closed. "Now, start talking, Slam or Jaz. Who are you and what's going on?"

TWENTY-TWO

Lari turned the Hummer around and drove west again. The activity on the other side of the border disappeared into the distance. She stole glances across at the woman in the passenger seat next to her, but said nothing. Jaz looked across at Lari, smiling shyly. "Hola Lari." Her voice was soft and heavily accented. "Me alegra encontrarme con vosotros." She smiled at Lari again.

"Oh, ummnn... I don't speak... what language is that?" Lari stammered.

"It's Spanish, beautiful. She said hello to you and that she's pleased to meet you," Dante explained. He turned to Slam. "Are you both Mexican or Spanish? And that fuss on the Mexican side of the border... that was you? They were chasing you? Why?"

"Oh, hello Jaz," Lari told her before Slam could answer Dante. "I'm pleased to meet you too... I think." She smiled uncertainly at Jaz.

"I'm waiting, Slam," Dante urged.

Slam looked out the window, then turned to face Dante. "We're Spanish. We were taking some Mexicans across into the USA and we got noticed by the Federales. They chased us, we stopped, jumped out and ran across the border into your truck."

"You did that on purpose."

"Yes. We can travel further and faster in a vehicle. We can run fast as you know... what do you say? Sprint? But we can't maintain that speed for too long a distance. We just wanted to put as much distance between us and them as possible. We saw your vehicle travelling along the road and decided to stop you."

"Did you know we were vampires before you ran into us?"

"No. But I realized very quickly. As soon as you stopped. That's why we ran to the side of the road and hid. I thought maybe we made a mistake stopping you."

"So, how far do you want us to take you before we let you out?" Dante didn't look any more relaxed, despite the explanations.

"As far as you can."

Dante sighed again. "Larissa has to feed soon. We'll stop to fuel up and she'll feed. It might be best for you to stay with us past that stop so we don't draw any unwarranted attention."

Slam nodded his head slightly. He tapped Jaz on the shoulder and she turned to look at him over the back of the seat. "Larissa tiene que alimentar. Vamos a esperar y seguir viajando con Dante y Larissa."

"Sí, muy bien." She beamed at Slam, then turned to face front again.

"Slam just told her we'll stop for you to feed and they'll keep travelling with us and she said it was okay," Dante told Lari. "Close enough translation for you?" he asked Slam who nodded.

"You understand Spanish?"

"Yes, I can understand and speak it," Dante answered. "Does Jaz speak any English?"

"Maybe a word or two. She's never had to learn."

"What do you mean? And tell me your story..."

Slam sighed deeply. "I was made a vampire in 1671. I was a renegade, raiding the settlements of New Spain. We raided this one town and there was this woman... She was in her house and when I threw the door open to demand her valuables, the words froze in my throat... She had compelled me, although I didn't know that then. I was frozen where I stood and she bit me. Then I awoke and it was the next day and I was a vampire. She was gone and so was my ship but I killed everyone left in that town, my hunger was so great. Then I burned the town and retreated to the jungles briefly. Over time, I learnt to be more discreet in feeding and I gathered a crew and found myself a new ship. I met Jaz in 1678. She was a settler in another town in New Spain that I raided. I fell in love with her beauty and turned her. We've been together ever since. We've been living in Mexico for many years now and while I learnt English, it wasn't necessary for Jaz... We transport Mexicans across the border to America but we don't stay here long and I can always translate for her if it's needed."

"Wow. That's quite a story. You were a pirate. But if you're both Spanish and from the 1600s, Slam and Jaz can't be your real names."

"They are. Slambrosious and Jacinta. We have modernized them."

"Okay."

"Why don't you tell me something about yourselves?"

Dante gave him a long searching look. "Okay. My name's Dante, and Lari is short for Larissa. I'm English, she's Australian. We're living here and travelling... This is a surfing holiday – that's why there's surfboards on the roof. That's about all there is to tell."

"I can feel how young she is... she still feeds often... Did you turn her?"

"Yes."

"Then you have a bond with her like I have with my Jaz."

Dante nodded slowly.

"You are young too... though not as young as your Lari... But much younger than us." Slam smiled at Dante. "It's your youth that frightened us when we stopped you. I can sense Lari's fear. We won't harm you and you won't harm us, yes?"

Again, Dante nodded. "Why did our youth frighten you?"

"Because it makes you unpredictable. You were frightened to encounter us and that fear could propel you to harm us where older vampires wouldn't necessarily be afraid to encounter us and might talk to us before they decided they wished to harm us." He smiled again at Dante. "I hope I explained myself then. English is my second language so I sometimes make mistakes."

"I understand. So, none of us wishes to harm the others."

"Yes, it is agreed."

"Yes." He turned to face the back of Lari's head. "Lari, take the Calexico turn-off just ahead. There'll be somewhere nearby to get fuel and for you to feed."

"'Kay, honey." She paused, then continued, "How do I say pleased to meet you in Spanish, Dante?"

"Me alegra encontrarme con vosotros."

"Me alegra encontrarme con vosotros, Jaz," she haltingly told the woman next to her.

Jaz smiled back at her, "Gracias."

TWENTY-THREE

Lari pulled into the truckstop and parked near the pumps. "Not a lot of people here, Dante," she told him. "Should I try to find someone or wait a bit longer?"

"I don't know, beautiful. It's up to you."

She frowned, turning to look at him in the back seat. "You get the fuel and I'll take a walk to the Ladies and think about it, okay?"

"Okay," he answered. Turning to face Slam, he continued, "You two wait here and don't do anything if you want us to take you further."

"Si," Slam answered.

Dante jumped out with Lari who handed him the Hummer's keys as she kissed his cheek. "Only you can hear me, beautiful. If you want to tell me something they can't hear, just say what you want silently like I'm doing now. Okay?" he told her.

Lari stared intently at him, and a few minutes later replied silently, "Okay, I can do that. I wanted to say something cheeky but my mind went blank." She smiled at Dante. "Okay, I'm going to check out the dinner menu," she laughingly told him loudly as she walked into the building.

Dante grinned back at her. "Good luck, beautiful." He slipped the keys into his pocket and started pumping the gas, staring into the vehicle at their unexpected passengers.

"I know it was a strange way to meet, but we really mean you know harm." Dante heard Slam's voice in his head. "Perhaps we can become friends."

"Perhaps," Dante answered him silently. "Will either of you need to feed soon?"

"No, we are good, but thank you for asking," Slam replied without speaking. Inside the Hummer, he turned to look out at Dante, smiling at him and nodding. "You are worried about and protective of your Lari. I understand. I have the same considerations for Jaz."

"Okay. I'm going to pay for the fuel now," he spoke out loud, hanging up the pump. Opening the rear door and leaning in, he added in a quieter tone, "We like to appear as human as possible, to not attract attention. We shall continue our conversation when I return."

Dante walked into the building to pay and returned a few minutes later accompanied by Lari and with a bag of takeaway food clutched in his hand. They resumed their seats in the Hummer and Lari immediately drove off.

"Were you able to feed, Larissa?" asked Slam.

"Yes, thank you," she answered him, smiling at him in the rear view mirror. Slam returned her smile. "Will either of you need to feed anytime soon?"

"No. We fed last week and won't need to feed again for a day or two," he replied.

"Oh, so how often do you need to feed then? Or am I being rude asking?" she quizzed him.

"No, it's alright. We usually need to feed every seven to ten days." Slam frowned as he looked across to Dante with the food on his lap. "May I ask why you have that?"

"Because Lari spoke loudly enough for others to hear when she talked of checking out the dinner menu, so I bought something while she was in the toilets. When she stepped out, I told her I'd already paid for the fuel and bought food so we could leave now. We live among humans, as part of their lives, so I'm extremely cautious about not being noticed, not attracting attention unduly."

"I see," Slam answered. He was quiet for a few miles, then continued, "We mostly live... what is that phrase? Ah, off the grid. We don't interact with humans unless we're transporting them or feeding from them. Or not very often do we interact in other ways. Your ways are much different to ours."

"Yes, I guess they are. Where do you both live? Do you maintain a house or are you always moving?"

"We have a home in a small town in Spain, on the outskirts of Portonovo. The home is somewhat isolated and very old. It has been ours for many, many years. There we keep our treasured belongings. We do not live there but we visit often. It is our... retreat? We have been resident in Mexico for a few years now. Transporting Mexicans to America has been profitable for us." He smiled at Dante. "You are still young. Your need to interact will lessen."

"Perhaps. But I know others your age who still choose to live as we do."

"Really? Where are these vampires? I have met very few in all my years. Most do not wish for any interaction, even with their own kind."

"They travel. I believe they are currently in Australia... where I met Lari."

"Ahhh... a coven, perhaps?"

"No. Simply two other couples who have a friendship."

"We do like to pair. Something to do with existing through eternity, perhaps."

"I think so," answered Dante. "I feel reborn since I found Lari."

"Oh, thank you, sweetie!" exclaimed Lari, smiling. "Sorry to interrupt then," she giggled.

Dante grinned, "It's okay, beautiful."

Jaz turned to look at Slam and spoke, "¿Qué está sucediendo, Slam?"

"Estoy describiendo nuestra casa en España y nuestra forma de vida."

"Eso está bien. Gracias." Jaz smiled at him and turned back around in her seat.

"She wanted to know what was happening and he told her what he's telling us and she's okay with that," Dante silently told Lari.

"I wish I could speak Spanish so I'd understand her too. The language sounds beautiful. Can I learn it, Dante?" Lari asked him telepathically.

"Yes. But not right now."

"Okay. I'll hold you to that."

"You were telling me about the way you live, Slam... Want to continue?" Dante returned to speaking out loud.

Slam nodded and continued, "In Mexico we have lived in a few different places... We move around. We have a boat that is moored in one of the harbours, but we do not live aboard when it is moored. It is for us to travel between countries." He grinned at Dante, "We wish not to attract the attention of the Federales while we are transporting people... but as you saw, sometimes it happens as it did tonight."

"What happened to your cargo of people tonight?"

Slam shrugged. "The Federales would have let them out of the truck and let them go home. They will not get to America today." He smiled, "But our fee is paid in advance and non-refundable, so I am satisfied."

TWENTY-FOUR

Lari drove through the night, stopping only to put more fuel in the Hummer. Slam and Jaz stayed with them and in the early hours of the morning, she pulled over on the outskirts of San Diego.

"I don't want to drive in the traffic, Dante," she told him as she turned off the engine. "Will you take over now?"

"We have never been to this zoo you are going to. May we accompany you? Jaz would very much like it, I think," Slam asked before Dante could answer Lari.

Dante sighed and looked thoughtfully at Slam. "Okay. Jump out and get in the front with me. The girls can have the back for a while."

Slam tapped Jaz on the shoulder and spoke to her, "Vamos a intercambiar asientos. Me sentaré donde usted está y usted se sentará donde estoy. Vamos a visitar el parque zoológico."

"Si," she answered him. All four got out of the Hummer and swapped seats. Once they were all back in the truck, Dante started the engine and drove off towards the zoo.

"Slam, why do you speak out loud to Jaz to translate for her? And why does she not ask you silently for the translations?" he asked as they drove.

"So that you know what we say. We have not enough trust between us yet for me to translate silently for her."

"Fair enough. Though you could still be saying other things to her that we can't hear."

"Yes, that is true, but I am not. There is no need. I wish to build some trust between us, to thank you for this assistance."

"Okay." They drove the rest of the distance to the zoo without discussion. Lari had the video camera out and was filming their journey. "Save some disk space for the zoo..." Dante told her as he parked the truck. "Or do you have a spare disk?"

"There's still an unused one, Dante," she told him as she switched off the camera and replaced the disk. "Wow, San Diego Zoo... I'm excited... I like zoos, Dante." They all got out of the Hummer and Dante armed the alarm.

"Oh, Dante! Their feet!" Lari exclaimed.

Dante looked down at Slam and Jaz's bare feet. "Oh, shit. You guys need some footwear." He frowned as he thought. "I know. We've got thongs in our duffels. You can both wear them. It won't matter if they're the wrong size." He disarmed the alarm, opened the back of the Hummer and reached for their duffels.

"Thongs?" queried Slam. "What are thongs?"

"They're rubber footwear..." he tried to explain as he rummaged through the two duffels. "Wait, I think they call them flip-flops in America," he added as he finally found them and thrust them at Slam and Jaz. "Here, put these on. You have to wear shoes to get in. Or I think you probably do."

Slam studied the two pairs of footwear, finally handing over the smaller pair to Jaz. "They are almost like wearing nothing, but they feel strange for me who has never worn anything like them," he said as he stepped into Dante's thongs. Jaz copied him and put Lari's thongs on her feet. He walked a few steps. "Yes, they are strange, but thank you."

"No problem. They generally prefer you to wear footwear in public places," Dante explained, putting away the duffels and arming the alarm for the second time.

They began walking to the entrance and Lari sniffed the air. "Animal blood doesn't do anything... I thought it would... before you made me a vampire. But it doesn't. I mean, I can sense it, but it doesn't stir the hunger."

"No. It is drinkable and I lived on it for many months in the jungle when I was first turned, but it is not pleasant nor satisfying," Slam told her.

Lari turned and raised her eyebrows at him. "I suppose you must have. I never realized when you told us you fled to the jungles, but you would've been young like me and needed to feed lots every day."

"Yes. Perhaps I even fed more because I was not satisfied by the blood."

"Oh, yes... maybe you did. There's no way to really know, is there?"

"No. My Jaz was able to feed from human blood from the first and her hunger was great for many months... I cannot say if it was greater than mine or not."

"I wish I understood her. It sounds beautiful when you speak Spanish to each other."

"Gracias. Perhaps we can teach you. Your Dante speaks our language. Maybe he would prefer to be the one to teach you."

"How long do you plan to travel with us, Slam?" Dante interrupted as they entered the zoo.

Slam paused and exchanged a look with Jaz. "Jaz wishes to learn some English so that she can speak with Lari. She has a longing for a woman friend, something she has not had for a very long time. I would like if we could travel with you for some weeks and grow a friendship. I like for Jaz to be happy and this would make her happy."

"Let me think about it while we look around the zoo," Dante answered.

"Yes. Perhaps Jaz and I should look around separately and reunite here with you after so that you have some time alone together?"

"Okay. Do you have a watch?"

"No."

"Do you have a mobile phone?"

"No. We have none of those things. They are unnecessary in our lives."

"Okay. Take my phone." Dante removed his phone from his pocket and set the alarm for three hours. "I've set the alarm for one o'clock. When it goes off, meet us back here."

Slam took the phone from him. "Thank you." He smiled at them both. "I hope we can travel more together. Enjoy the zoo." Turning to Jaz, he slipped Dante's phone into his back pocket and reached for her hand. "Venido, Jaz. Exploremos el parque zoológico."

"See you in three hours, Slam, Jaz!" Lari exclaimed with a smile. "Are you going to let them travel more with us, Dante?" she asked as the two couples walked away from each other.

"Let me think about it. Look around and we'll talk about it a bit later on."

"Okay. I'd like to get to know Jaz. She's really pretty... and I'd like to learn Spanish, too," she told him. "Oh, look at that!" she exclaimed, running off towards an animal pen.

Dante smiled as he followed her, turning once to glance at Slam and Jaz strolling along another path.

TWENTY-FIVE

Three hours later Dante and Lari were back just inside the entrance to the zoo waiting for Slam and Jaz. They heard them before they saw them. The alarm on Dante's phone was chiming as they walked into view.

"Give me the phone and I'll turn that off," Dante told him as they reached him.

"Si. I didn't know how to use it so I couldn't turn it off. Sorry," Slam smiled sheepishly as he handed Dante the phone. "I don't wish to rush you but we would like to know. Have you thought on if we can continue to travel with you?"

Dante sighed and glanced at Lari, who's eyes pleaded with him. "It appears that Lari would like to get to know Jaz as well, so the answer is yes, you can."

"Gracias," he grinned at Dante and turned quickly to Jaz. "Podemos continuar el viaje con Dante y Lari."

Jaz grinned back at him and then quickly spun around to hug Lari. "Seremos amigos, Lari."

"I don't know what you said, but amigos is friends, right?" Lari asked, laughing and hugging her back.

"Yes, it is, beautiful," Dante told her with a smile. "She wants to be friends with you."

"Oh, I want to be friends with her, too," Lari told him. "What was it she said?"

"Seremos amigos," Dante told her.

"Seremos amigos, Jaz," Lari told her with a smile.

"Si, si," answered Jaz, lunging forward and hugging her again. "¿Cuál es la palabra inglesa para los amigos?" she asked Slam.

"Friends," he told her.

Turning to Jaz, she said in her heavily accented voice, "Friends."

"Yes, friends," Lari answered.

"Okay, now that we've sorted that out, how about we continue driving?" Dante asked. "And Slam, you don't have to translate out loud for Jaz, either. If we're going to have trust, it has to start somewhere."

"Gracias," nodded Slam.

"Woohoo! Let's go, but you get to drive through San Diego coz I don't want to," Lari told Dante. "Can we go to Hollywood on the way?"

"Yes, we can. When did you decide you wanted to go there?"

"About three years ago, before I ever knew you," she retorted, sticking her tongue out at him. "I want to go to lots of places in Hollywood, too."

Dante laughed. "Okay, Hollywood it is." Turning to Slam, he continued, "Sure you want to keep travelling with us? You'll have to play human a lot."

"Si, I understand. It is what Jaz wants."

"Okay. Then let's go. We can be in Hollywood in a few hours."

"We get a hotel room, okay? Coz I meant it when I said there was lots I wanted to see. And I'm kinda sick of being in the car."

"Yes, we can do that, too."

She threw her arms around his neck and kissed him. "I love you, Dante. You're the best." Releasing him, she turned to Slam, "Did you and Jaz like the zoo? I loved it."

"Si, it was very good. Now we go to Hollywood and stay in a hotel?"

"Yes, just for a couple of days so we can do some sightseeing. Then we're heading to a beach called Mavericks where we can surf. Can either of you surf?" she asked.

"No. We have never surfed. But we can look around while you surf, yes?"

"Yeah, that's a good idea. You can do that." She spun back to Dante, "I'm so excited! Hollywood in a few hours and surfing in a few days."

"Yes, beautiful, but not if we keep standing around here talking. Time for us to get back on the road, chatterbox."

"'Kay." She turned to Jaz and took her hand. "C'mon Jaz, we're going now."

Jaz glanced at Slam who nodded, silently translating their conversation for her. Nodding in reply, she smiled and walked with Lari out of the zoo, Dante and Slam following close behind.

TWENTY-SIX

It was pouring with rain as they turned onto West Sunset Boulevard. Lari was wide-eyed, the video camera pointing out the window. "Wow, Dante, I'm so excited! This is Hollywood! I want to go to that Chinese Theatre... I can't remember what it's called. And I want to see all those stars' handprints in the footpath. And there's so many other things too, but I can't remember them all right now," she squealed in joy. "I wish it wasn't raining. Do you think it'll stop soon?"

"I don't know, beautiful," Dante answered. "Any ideas where you wanted to stay?"

"Uh, no... but somewhere nice would be good."

"Okay." Dante frowned as he drove. The Sunset Tower loomed ahead. "This one looks good. Would you like to stay here? It's close to most of the things I think you want to see."

"Yeah, it looks good to me, too."

"Okay, then we'll check in here and work out where we're going after that." He turned into the hotel entrance and parked in a temporary parking spot. "Slam, let Jaz know we're checking in here. Wait in the truck and I'll be right back as soon as I have us checked in." He jumped out and strolled in the entrance.

"Will Dante get accommodation for us also?" Slam asked Lari.

"Yes, he will. That's okay, isn't it?"

"Oh, yes. Thank you." He turned to face Jaz, smiling as he silently told her what was happening. "Jaz thanks you also," he finally told Lari.

"No problem. Oh look, here's Dante," she said as he returned.

He spoke in a voice too low for any but them to hear. "Okay, fellow vamps, we have a two bedroom suite so we can all stay together." At a normal volume, he continued, "The valet has the keys and he's going to park this, so let's get our luggage and boards." Lari, Jaz and Slam all got out. "Now, Lari and I have luggage, but you two don't. You're going to need some shoes if you're travelling with us, and you could probably use some spare clothes too. Some shopping might be in order for this afternoon, before we do any sightseeing," he told them.

"Oh, but it's okay to check in, isn't it?" Lari asked him.

"Yes, that's done. We'll take our bags and our boards up to our suite. We can shower and change if you like, and then we can do some shopping with Slam and Jaz." He turned to Slam. "Is that okay with you?"

"Si, that is fine with me." Continuing in a voice too low for human ears, he added, "We don't usually mix with humans long enough to need to worry about these things, but Jaz is always happy to have new clothes and shoes so I see no problem with this."

The valet came over as they removed the boards from the roof of the SUV. Dante grabbed both their duffels from inside the vehicle, handing them to Slam and taking hold of one board. Lari hung onto the other.

"Are you ready for me to park the vehicle, sir?" asked the valet.

"Yes, thank you." Dante tipped him and they all started walking into the hotel together. Riding in the lift up to their floor, Dante asked, "How do you pay for things, Slam? Do you have a credit card or must it be cash?"

"I have a credit card. My bank is in Spain and my card is Spanish, but it will work fine here."

"Great. I just wondered coz you said you don't mix and you don't have a mobile phone or a watch and I didn't know if that meant you didn't have a bank account either." He shrugged and smiled.

"No, I have a bank account with a credit card attached. It is necessary in today's world," he grinned back. "I only have what I need. I do have a watch but I left it in the truck we left behind in Mexico. I don't like to wear them and I had taken it off." He laughed again. "Well, perhaps I don't have a watch anymore. I will need another. The mobile phone has never been necessary so I don't have one."

"How do you arrange your cargo then? I mean, how do they get in touch with you and how do you get in touch with whoever it is you need to get in touch with on this side?" he asked Slam.

"There are certain bars and other places where those who wish our services go to in order to find us. We don't meet anyone on this side. There are probably some who do, but not us. We merely drop them off when they are on this side of the border and then we leave. We are paid in full before departure so there is really no need for us to maintain contact after we have delivered them to this country."

Dante swiped the keycard for their suite and opened the door. "Oh, okay." He smiled and continued, "What about the ones who don't make it to this side, like the ones you left behind last night?"

Slam grinned back. "There are no refunds. There is risk in this transport and they know this. Most make it across with us. Some don't." He stepped back to allow Jaz and Lari to enter first.

"Oh wow! This is really nice, Dante!" Lari exclaimed as she walked in and leaned her surfboard against one of the walls. She looked in each of the bedrooms, returning to the first and tossing her bag onto the bed. "Oh, I'm sorry Slam, but we're having this bedroom. There's a bath. I think I'd really love to have a big bubbly bath," she called out.

Dante joined her in the room and tossed his bag on the bed. "You have your bath, sweetie," he told her, planting a kiss on her cheek.

"We take the other room, Dante?" Slam asked from the living space.

"Oh yes, sorry. Go for it," Dante answered, coming out of the bedroom. "Lari's going to have a bath. Maybe Jaz would like a shower too?"

Slam nodded. "It seems that she does. We will freshen up and be ready for shopping soon."

"No worries." Dante sat on the couch and turned on the television.

Slam sat next to him. "You don't mind if I sit with you?"

"No, go ahead. I'm just going to watch some TV while I wait for Lari to get ready. Why didn't you compel the officers that stopped you last night?"

"Gracias. There were too many. Had it been just one or two Federales, then we would've compelled them to let us continue, but there were more than four vehicles and the helicopter. It was better and safer just to run."

"Okay, I get that." Dante flicked through the channels, finally settling on one.

"The television fascinates me. I remember the first televisions. Do you also?" asked Slam.

"Yeah, I do." He looked at Slam. "I hadn't thought about them in years. TV has certainly made some huge advances since then."

"Yes, it has. Sometimes it is hard to keep up with technology and there are times I feel my years. It can be overwhelming at times."

"Yeah, I suppose it can be. You're much older than me and there's been much more change for you than me."

"Yes. From sailing ships and horse and carriage to the big cruise ships of today, and the aeroplanes and trains and cars and buses." He shook his head in amazement. "Just the transport changes have been so many. There are times I wonder and fear my future."

Dante looked at him thoughtfully. "You've given me something to think about, Slam. Eternity can seem even longer if you start to look ahead."

"Yes, better to live in the now. Even the past can be too long."

TWENTY-SEVEN

Just over an hour later they caught the lift down to the lobby. Leading the way, Dante walked over to the concierge desk. "Excuse me. Do you know where my friends can buy some new clothes? Their luggage has gone astray and they really need new clothes and shoes."

"Good thinking, Dante," Lari told him silently.

"Yes, sir. Did you wish to find something in walking distance or are you willing to drive?"

"I'd prefer walking distance if that's possible."

The concierge pulled out a tourist map and drew a circle on it. "This is where we are now," he told Dante as he drew another circle. "This is the Hollywood and Highland Center," he told him, drawing a line connecting the two circles. "It's about two miles from here, a long walk, but you'll find many shops there and I'm sure your friends will be able to find clothes and shoes to suit. There are also other shops along the way. If you decide to drive, there is a large carpark attached, so parking shouldn't be an issue."

"Thanks. We're fine to walk. May I take this map?"

The concierge handed over the map. "Yes, please do. Enjoy your walk and your shopping trip." He handed Dante a card with a phone number printed on it. "This is the hotel number. If you wish to have a car from our car service collect you rather than walk back, please call and ask to speak to the concierge to arrange it."

"Thanks. We may do that." Dante smiled at him, before rejoining the others and walking towards the entrance.

"Sir! Sir!" the concierge called as they walked away.

"Yes?" Dante turned to face him.

"Would you like to hire some umbrellas? It's rather wet out there."

"Uh, yes. Good idea. Thanks." Dante returned to the desk and completed the paperwork. He returned to the others and handed Slam one of the umbrellas.

Together they walked out the entrance and into the rain. A few hours later they returned to the hotel laden with shopping bags and a pair of duffels similar to Dante and Lari's. They returned the umbrellas to the concierge and went directly to their suite.

"Well, that was productive," Dante told them as he dropped onto the sofa and turned on the television.

"Dante! You're not going to zone out on that are you?" asked Lari as she followed him in, Jaz and Slam just behind her.

"C'mon. You made me go shopping for clothes and shoes all afternoon. I deserve a break," he complained.

"All afternoon? Like it was only two hours or something. Not long at all." She walked over and lightly cuffed him on the shoulder. "Fine. I'm going to check out Jaz's new things with her." Lari spun round and smiled at Jaz. "Can you translate that for me Slam?" she asked him, still smiling at Jaz.

"Si," he answered Lari. He translated silently for her. Jaz smiled at Lari and nodded her head, gesturing with her hand for Lari to follow her as she walked into her room. Lari followed, and Slam joined Dante on the sofa.

"Hey," Dante greeted him. "So, when will you and Jaz need to feed? I'm okay tonight but Lari still feeds daily so she'll want something soon."

"We are okay also tonight. Perhaps tomorrow would be good."

"Yeah, tomorrow would be good for me too."

"How long will we stay here, Dante?"

"I've checked us in for two days. I think that will be enough to satisfy Lari. Then we're off to Mavericks. You still want to stay with us?"

"Si," Slam stretched. "Jaz is happy to be making a friend. You don't mind that we stay?"

"No, I don't mind. Lari's pretty happy to have Jaz around too."

"That is good. At our next destination I will pay for the accommodation, yes? I am not short of money."

"You don't have to." Dante gave a short laugh. "I'm not short of money, either."

"No, but I would like to. It is okay?"

"Yeah, sure. You can pay next time if you want." Dante took a deep breath before he continued, "What are you going to do if you're not trafficking people, Slam? I mean, that was your source of income, wasn't it?"

"It was some of it. I have much money in the bank, and I have investments. We transport people for something to do. It fills our time and provides more money, and there is an element of risk that reminds me of when I was a renegade."

"Okay."

"What is it that you do, Dante?"

"Not much, really. Sometimes I further my studies at universities or similar and other times I've been a soldier, and I've worked in various fields, but right now, we are living off my investments." Dante smiled. "Like you, I have money in the bank and investments."

"What did you do before you were turned?"

"I was a gentleman of leisure," Dante laughed. "No, I'm sorry. That's not strictly true. I had been away to university and had just returned when it happened so I never started work anywhere. It was the 1800s."

"What happened to the vampire that turned you?"

"I don't know. Like yours, he didn't stick around. Well, he hung around a bit longer than the vampire that turned you did, but only long enough to teach me what I needed to know to survive."

"I learnt that in the jungles and over the years I have learnt more, but you are correct, she who turned me never taught me anything, like I taught my Jaz and I'm sure you teach Lari."

"Yes. It's harder coming to terms with the changes when you don't even understand what is happening. Lari was prepared in a way."

"Perhaps. Do you mean your Lari knew you were to change her?"

"Yes. She knew what I was and she got terminally ill, so she asked that I change her and I did."

"She knew you were a vampire before you changed her?"

"Yes. I didn't want to change her but in the end I saw it was the only way."

"I am astounded. Jaz found out what I was after she, too, was a vampire. I could not imagine telling her before."

"I couldn't imagine not telling Lari," Dante told him and conversation over, they both sat quietly, absorbing the new information.

TWENTY-EIGHT

Lari had a list of nightclubs she wanted to visit so they spent that evening making their way around the various clubs. Unseen in a dark corner of the Viper Room, Lari drank from an unsuspecting victim.

"Oh Dante, that blood had some kind of buzz to it!" she told him after, in a voice too low for anyone else to hear.

"Probably the alcohol in it."

"Can I get drunk off it?"

Dante laughed, "Not unless you drained them... even then, probably not."

"Oh, well," she licked her lips. "It did have a strange after-taste. Not bad, just strange."

"That's what happens when you hunt in places like this," he told her with a grin.

Jaz was wide-eyed for the entire evening, clutching tightly to Slam's hand for most of it. Slam explained that neither of them had ever been anywhere like it before. They returned to the hotel in the early hours, long after midnight. Lari immediately began teaching Jaz some English, while Jaz responded by teaching Lari some Spanish. Dante and Slam watched television and continued getting to know each other better. The sun came up as the two couples retired to their bedrooms for some alone time.

The following day was consumed with sightseeing around Hollywood. It had stopped raining, the sun was shining and Lari was bounding with energy. She dragged Dante from one end of Hollywood Boulevard to the other, found her way to Melrose Avenue in Beverly Hills and then back to Sunset Strip. Jaz and Slam trailed along with Slam silently translating for Jaz so that she and Lari could communicate beyond the limited words they'd taught each other. Clutching bags of souvenirs, clothes and shoes, Lari danced around Dante when they finally returned to their suite.

"That was just the best ever day, Dante! I had so much fun!" she sang. Twirling to face Slam and Jaz, she asked them, "Did you like it, too?"

"Yes," answered Slam, smiling. "Although to be honest, I think Jaz was more excited by the shopping than I was. I did like seeing the city. I have not been here before."

"Cool!" She ran into the bedroom and dropped her shopping bags on the floor before returning to the living area where Dante was sprawled on the sofa. Jaz and Slam had disappeared into their bedroom. "How much longer are we here for, Dante?"

"We check out tomorrow morning. I thought that was long enough, but if you want us to stay longer, I can arrange it."

"Nah, I'm about done, I think. I wanna surf now. How far away is Mavericks from here?" She straddled him, leaning down to punctuate her sentences with kisses.

"Not sure, exactly, but not too far away," he answered her between kisses.

"So we can be surfing by tomorrow night?" she asked, sitting up.

"I don't see why not. You'll want to stick around to surf there a while, won't you?"

She grinned, "Of course. Why wouldn't I? And why do you ask?" She kissed him again, her hands sneaking in under his T-shirt.

"Because Slam told me yesterday that he'd like to pay for our next accommodations and if we're going to stay there a while so we can surf, then we should probably check in somewhere near there."

"Oh, okay. Yes, we should get rooms somewhere near. It's been such a long time since I went surfing, I think I'll want to surf for days."

Dante's hands slid over her hips, caressing her butt as he kissed her deeply. "We should probably move into the bedroom... have some consideration for our new friends... What do you think?"

"Oh, I think that sounds like a great idea... especially if we're going to get naked."

"Yeah, naked is good. Let's go." He picked her up and carried her into the bedroom. Reaching the bed, he threw her down onto it, stripping his clothes as she did the same. Flinging her legs around his hips, she pulled him down onto her, her hands reaching round his neck and drawing him close as she kissed him passionately. "I love you, beautiful," he murmured in between kisses, slipping inside her.

"Oh, I love you," she answered him. "So, so much."

TWENTY-NINE

"I'm thirsty, Dante," she told him as the evening grew late.

"Yes, I think I'd like to feed also. Slam told me last night that he and Jaz would probably like to feed tonight as well. We should probably split up to do it. Could be a bit noticeable if four of us feed at the same time and difficult to find somewhere all of us could feed at the same time."

"Any ideas where?"

"No. There's plenty of dark alleys. I'm sure we can find people out alone here. That's one good thing about a big city. It is easier to feed in a way."

Lari knocked on the door to Jaz and Slam's room. "We're going out to feed."

"Wait, please," Slam answered, opening the door. "We wish to feed also."

"Okay," Lari told him. "Dante thinks it would be best if we split up to feed."

"Yes, he is correct. But we will leave with you, if you don't mind. We are not comfortable with needing to communicate with the humans or familiar with what is considered normal. So if we could meet outside the hotel and return together, we would appreciate it."

"Yeah, that's cool. We can do that."

"Gracias. Jaz is showering and will be dressed shortly."

"No problems." Lari smiled at him and wandered over to the sofa where she snuggled with Dante waiting for Slam and Jaz to be ready.

A short while later they walked out the front entrance together. "We shall go this way, Slam," Dante told him, speaking very softly, pointing down the street. "What if you go the other?"

"Yes. I think that is a good idea. If we return first, we shall wait until you arrive before we return to our room. If you return first, will you wait for us?"

"Yeah," he looked down the street. "Do you see that café there?" he asked, pointing to a café about half a block away.

"Yes, I see it." Slam looked puzzled.

"We'll meet there. If you get there first, just order coffee and wait. We'll do the same if we're first." He smiled at Slam. "Looks normal to wait for someone in a café, but not to just hang around on the street."

Slam nodded, "I understand. That is where we will wait or look for you."

"Great. Happy hunting," he told them with a smile.

"Gracias. Happy hunting to you also." Slam smiled, and taking Jaz's hand began walking down the street. Suddenly they blurred and disappeared.

Lari shook her head. "Wow, Dante. Is that what we look like to vampire eyes when we speed up?" she asked him silently.

"Yes," he answered her.

"To human eyes as well?"

Smiling indulgently, he answered, "No, to them we just vanish. Shall we also?"

"Yeah, time to feed," she replied.

Together they strolled in the opposite direction to Jaz and Slam. Out of sight of the hotel entrance, they suddenly sped up and disappeared, slowing down in downtown Los Angeles.

"Is this a good spot, do you think?" she asked him as they slowed.

Dante looked around. "Plenty of dark alleys. Look around for someone by themselves, or a couple. We can compel them to go into an alley where we can feed undiscovered."

Lari looked around thoughtfully. "Where are we?"

"Downtown L.A."

"Oh, really?" She slowly turned full circle. "I suppose, it's full of office type buildings. I thought it would look different. I don't know why."

He laughed. "Stop sightseeing and start hunting."

She grinned back at him. "Yeah, yeah... I'm doing it. You could do the hunting, y'know..."

"I didn't mean that I wouldn't but if both of us are hunting we have a better chance of finding something."

"I know. I'm just teasing." She laughed and poked him in the ribs. "Sometimes you're just too serious." Suddenly she snapped to attention, spining round to look down the street. "Dante... do you see them?"

"Yes. They just turned into that alley. Perfect. Let's do it." Together they sped up again and caught up to the drunk couple staggering down the dark lane.

Dante tapped the man's shoulder and he turned to look at Dante. "Hi. You won't remember any of this. You're going to sleep now," Dante told the man, staring into his eyes. The man closed his eyes and Dante caught him as he went limp. Dante began feeding almost immediately.

The girl looked at him, confused. "What?" she began, her voice sounding panicked.

"Look at me," Lari told her as she grabbed the girl's face and turned it towards her. The girl stared as Lari compelled her. "You won't remember anything. You're going to sleep and when you wake, the last thing you'll remember is walking into this lane."

The girl slumped and Lari caught her before she hit the ground. Immediately she, too, began feeding.

THIRTY

The next morning they were packed and ready to leave an hour before checkout time.

"Okay, are we all ready to leave?" Dante asked them as they gathered in the living area. They all nodded. "Right then. Let's go." He led the way out and into the lift. He and Lari carried a surfboard each, along with their duffels, while Jaz and Slam each carried a duffel.

Down at the reception desk, he handed in the room key and requested his SUV. They waited at the front entrance for the SUV to be brought around. "Slam, we've gotten to know each other better now. You can sit with Jaz in the back and Lari can sit with me in the front. Is that okay with you?"

"Si, that is good. Gracias," Slam answered, smiling. "Podemos sentarnos juntos en el asiento trasero," he told Jaz.

Jaz smiled back at him. "Thank you, Dante," she told him in her thickly accented English.

"No problem. Your English is getting much better, Jaz," he answered. The valet brought the Hummer around and they tossed their bags in the back while Dante fastened the boards to the roof. Slam and Jaz climbed into the back seat and Lari hopped into the front on the passenger side. Dante grinned at her as he got into the driver's seat. "I take it I'm the driver again."

"Of course. There's way too much traffic and stuff for me to do any driving." She leaned over to kiss his cheek. "If you want, I can take over when we get onto the open road." She paused and frowned. "There will be more open roads, won't there?"

Starting the engine and driving off, he grinned back at her. "If by open road you mean the interstates, then, yes, we'll be back on the I-5 and heading north soon. Maverick's is near San Francisco, in Pillar Point Harbor, just north of Half Moon Bay. I looked it up while you were packing this morning."

"Cool. We can go to San Francisco then, too."

"Any more places you want to include on the visit list?" Dante asked her.

"Probably. You did say we didn't have a schedule or time limit on the trip."

"Yeah, I did. Why do I think I'm gonna end up regretting that?"

Lari thumped his shoulder and glared at him. "I'll hurt you..." she threatened.

Dante laughed. "Yeah, I know. I'm used to it now." She thumped him again. Sensing confusion emanating from Slam, he added, "It's okay, Slam. This is one of Lari's ways of showing me love."

The traffic got dense and they crawled to a stop. "So how far away is Maverick's?" Lari asked.

"About six hours. Probably more if there's a lot of traffic like this."

"Oh, so we won't get there till evening." Lari frowned, then smiled. "We can go night surfing!"

"Do you think that's a good idea? It's supposed to be a pretty dangerous beach and you've never surfed there before."

Lari rolled her eyes at him. "Are you serious? I mean, can I die there? Surfing?"

Dante sighed. "Okay, I didn't think it through." He glanced at her and smiled. "I guess it's not so dangerous for you, then. But, you can come off your board, and it could end up smashed to pieces."

"That would suck. But if it happens, I just have to buy a new board."

"I'd like to see you buy a board late at night, and that Winton of yours is pretty special to you, isn't it?"

She stared out at the traffic, a serious and thoughtful expression on her face. "Yeah, okay. It is kinda special. Can we stop somewhere on the way then and buy another board? One I can use tonight to surf?" She frowned at him. "Why didn't you think of that before we left home? I could've bought a new board before we left and this one could've stayed home."

"You didn't suggest night surfing at a dangerous beach before we left home."

"Okay. So, can we stop and get another board? Coz I am surfing tonight and if it's on the board I have now, well... I'll just have to hope it doesn't smash."

"You're determined to surf tonight?" he asked.

"Yes," she answered firmly.

"Well then, I guess we'll stop and get one somewhere. Let me just think where."

She leaned over and kissed his cheek. "Thank you, Dante."

THIRTY-ONE

They arrived at Maverick's just as the sun was setting. Dante had circled around and found a surf shop in Studio City, buying a new board for each of them before they returned to travelling north and got onto the I-5. So now there were four boards strapped to the roof of the Hummer. Lari had taken over the driving once they were on the interstate, pulling over and swapping back into the passenger seat just after they took the turn-off to San Francisco. Dante parked the Hummer at the top of the cliffs and they all got out and walked down to the beach.

"Check it out, Dante! It looks great. And the waves don't look too big tonight." Lari sounded excited. They watched the sun slip below the horizon and the stars appear.

"You will go out and surf tonight?" Slam asked her.

"Yeah. What will you guys do?"

"We will stay and watch. Perhaps later we may wander." He turned to Dante. "We are not staying in a hotel tonight?"

"No. We can find somewhere to check into tomorrow. Do you want a hotel tonight?"

"No, we are fine. We have not ever stayed in a hotel before this trip." Slam smiled. "Jaz wishes to improve on her English, so I will teach her more while you surf."

"Cool. Are you going to surf too, Dante?" Lari asked.

"Maybe. We'll see."

"Okay. Do you think I better put my wetsuit on or will I get away with just my bikini?"

"What do you mean?"

"Well, do you think anyone human is going to see me surfing and wonder why I don't need a wetsuit?"

"Good point. I don't know. Wear the wetsuit."

She wrinkled her nose. "I hate wetsuits." Rolling her eyes, she continued, "Don't look at me like that. I'll wear it. Would much rather be wearing just my bikini, but I won't do that." She sighed. "When did you ever see me in a wetsuit back when we met? Some of those days were pretty cold, y'know."

"Yeah, and you were human and got goosebumps and shivered. I don't think you're gonna get goosebumps and shiver now."

"Yeah, well you didn't and I never noticed."

"No, you just remarked about a million times about how cold I always felt."

She pulled a face at him. "I did not. You told me why you were always cold only a few days after we met."

"Oh, all right. There's no-one but us here and it's night, so don't wear it then."

"Thanks, honey," she beamed at him.

"I don't know why you asked since you obviously didn't want to wear it."

Lari shrugged and smiled at him.

"Excuse me, but you knew Dante was a vampire very shortly after you met? How long before he turned you?"

Lari pulled a face. "Gee, I'm not sure exactly. It was months later coz it was after my birthday."

Slam looked startled. "You never thought to betray his confidence?"

Lari looked horrified. "No! Why would I want to do that?"

"I am truly astonished." He turned to Dante. "You go to such great lengths to blend in with humans, yet you told your secret within days of meeting Lari."

"It was different. She was different. I just knew that." Dante stumbled over his explanation. "We fell in love. We both knew it."

"I am still astonished. Also that you never once betrayed him in all the months after he shared his secret." He looked again at Dante. "How long did you intend to wait before you turned her?"

"I didn't. I wanted her to stay human. Then she got ill and she was going to die."

"And I asked him to change me. I made him do it."

"I was reluctant, but when I saw she really wanted me to change her, and I knew I would lose her if I didn't... well, I had no choice... I just couldn't imagine spending the rest of eternity without her."

"I felt that way about Jaz, but I turned her and then told her what I am, what she is now."

"Didn't you think to give her a choice?"

"No. I didn't."

"Perhaps it was just a different time. After all, you changed Jaz in the 1600s and I changed Lari only last year."

"Perhaps." Slam sounded unconvinced.

"Well, enough of this interesting conversation. I'm gonna go put my bikini on and head into the water. Dante, you wanna pull my new board off the roof for me?"

"Sure."

"Thanks, honey," she told him, as she ran back to the Hummer to get her bikini and change.

"What if Jaz had reacted badly to you changing her, Slam?" Dante asked him.

"I don't know. I never thought of it, and she was pleased to find she would stay beautiful for eternity."

"Lari has..." he paused, looking for the right word, "opinions. I could never make a decision like that for her. She'd never forgive me, even if I chose what she would've wanted."

"When you told me before that she was aware she was to be changed, I did not understand that she knew you were a vampire for some time before you changed her. I thought you informed her immediately before you changed her."

Dante shook his head. "No. I told her not long after we met. It was something I needed to do before our relationship could develop."

"You live very differently to us. You pretend to be human, but you are vampires. It is not necessary to live as humans. Do you not tire of the pretense?"

"No." He sighed. "Well, maybe sometimes. But I... I can't imagine living any other way. To be cast adrift through eternity just doesn't appeal to me. Living like this keeps me feeling anchored to the world."

"I think I understand. But, for Jaz and I, our times of pretending to be human are limited and we do not have human lifestyles. We embrace what we are."

Dante smiled. "We live very differently." He glanced up towards the Hummer. "I better go get that board for her before she comes back all ready to surf and finds me still standing here and her board still on the roof." He ran to the Hummer and removed the two new boards, carrying them back to Slam and Jaz on the beach. Lari joined them a few minutes later, wearing her bikini and carrying a towel.

"Thanks, honey," she told Dante, handing him the towel, grabbing her new board from it's bag and heading for the water.

THIRTY-TWO

Lari surfed for the next half hour while Dante, Slam and Jaz remained on the beach watching her.

"She loves this surfing?" asked Slam.

"Yes. She's good at it. We spent a lot of time at the beach when she was still human."

"And you surf too?"

"Yes. I don't think I'm as good as her, but I like it. There's a kind of freedom in riding the waves."

"I think I prefer to travel over the water in a boat."

Dante grinned at him. "Boats are good. I don't mind sailing. I think Lari would like it, too. I should take her one day."

None of them noticed the young man standing on the cliffs, taking photos of Lari as she surfed.

"How long will she surf tonight?"

"I don't know. It's been months since she's been surfing and she used to surf nearly every day, so it could be a while."

"Will you join her?"

"Maybe. It looks like she's having fun out there." At that moment, she disappeared into the wave. "Damn. She's gone under."

"She's fallen off the board?"

"Yes. Kind of." Dante frowned as he stared out over the water, scanning for Lari.

"She will lose her new board?"

"No. She has a leg rope, so she'll still have her board." He stood up. "She should've surfaced. I can't see her."

"She cannot drown. There is no need to fear." Slam tried to reassure Dante.

"Yes. I know. But she may have been knocked unconscious and she'll be frightened if she has and she comes to and finds herself underwater. She hasn't experienced anything like that before."

"Ah, yes. I forgot how young she is. She is like an infant in terms of our lifespan." He joined Dante standing and looking out over the water. "Can you see her yet?"

The photographer on the clifftop was still taking photos of Lari's board floating on the surface, her body invisible in the dark water. Intent on trying to find Lari, no-one had yet noticed him.

"I'm going in to get her," Dante said, removing his shoes and moving quickly into the water. He swam out to her board while the photographer on the clifftop continued taking photos.

Reaching her board, he followed the leg rope to her unconscious body. He dragged her to the surface and onto the board. Swimming back to shore, pushing the board in front of him, he caught a glimpse of the camera's flash on the clifftop.

As they reached the shore, Lari came round and lifted her head from the board. "Dante? What happened?" she asked, as he gave the board one last shove into the shore and kneeled down beside her.

"You got knocked out. You can't drown but you can be knocked unconscious. I was afraid you'd be freaked out if you came to underwater, so I swam out to get you."

She sat up and unhooked her leg rope. "Thanks. I probably would've freaked." She leaned forward and kissed him. "Think I'll have a break. Surf more later, maybe."

Out of the corner of his eye, Dante caught sight of the flash again. "What is that?" he asked, staring up towards the clifftops.

"What's what?" she asked him, puzzled.

"Up there. On the clifftop. There's some kind of light going off." The camera flashed. "There it is again."

Lari looked to where Dante was pointing as the camera flashed repeatedly in quick succession. "It's a flash. From a camera. Someone's taking pictures," she told him. "You don't think they saw me in the water looking drowned, do you?"

Dante sat in the shallow water beside her. "Shit. Shit, shit, shit." He shook his head. "I saw the flash when I was getting you out of the water. Whoever it is was taking pictures of you after you came off the board. Probably before too. I just didn't realize."

Slam walked over to join them. "Excuse me, but we heard your conversation. This person with the camera, he must lose his pictures. He can't have these pictures."

"Yeah." Dante looked up at the clifftop again. "He's gone. I think he knows we saw him."

"He is not one of us. I would've sensed it that close."

Dante's eyes widened. "You can sense our kind from further away than us."

Slam nodded. "Yes, it appears so. But he was not one of our kind. And we must find him and remove his pictures. He, too, may be a problem."

"How are we going to do that?" Dante frowned, his eyes scanning the clifftop.

"Have you never tracked before?"

Dante looked at Slam and shook his head. "No."

"Then I will show you both. Put your boards away and join us at the top of the cliff where he was taking his pictures. Jaz and I will go there now." Slam sped off towards the clifftop, Jaz rising from the sand and racing with him.

"I'm sorry, Dante. This was all my fault."

"No. It was a random thing we could never have planned for. Let's put the boards away and learn to track. I hope we can just take the camera and get the pictures before anyone else sees them. I'd rather not kill anyone." He kissed her. "It's not your fault."

THIRTY-THREE

They joined Slam and Jaz at the top of the cliff. "This is where he stood," Slam told them as they reached him. "Sniff. Smell his scent."

"How do you know that's his scent?" Lari asked.

"It is the freshest scent here," Slam answered. "Please, do as I ask."

Dante and Lari did as he instructed. "Oh, I can smell him," Lari exclaimed.

"Know that scent. Find it elsewhere here."

Lari circled, sniffing. Soon she walked off a short distance. "He went in this direction." She thought about it. "Or he came from this direction." She turned to look at Slam. "How do I know which?"

"That is harder. The fresher scent will be the scent from when he left, but if he was not here long, there will be very little difference and it will be harder to distinguish." Slam turned to Dante. "Are you going to find his scent also?"

Dante looked reluctantly at him. "Yeah, I guess I am." He took a few steps toward the scent. "I'm not comfortable about this."

"It must be done."

"I know." He sniffed, moving closer to where Lari was circling.

Suddenly she stopped. "Here! Dante! Slam! Jaz! This is fresher. This is the way he ran when he left."

Slam nodded. "Yes, that is the direction that Jaz and I decided he went."

"Oh... Well, why didn't you just tell us that?" Lari pouted and complained petulantly.

"Because you needed to learn to track a scent. You cannot do that if I just tell you where he went. You must do it yourself to learn." He smiled to soften his words. "You have a gift for it."

Lari stared thoughtfully. "Yeah. Okay, then. So are we going to trail after him now or is there more learning?"

"We will track him. You must keep searching for his scent also. It will be harder if he has travelled through areas with many people or where many others have also travelled recently. We will communicate with our minds."

"Why communicate with our minds?" asked Dante.

"So that we can concentrate on tracking and so that we can move faster than human eyes and they will not hear our voices."

"Okay. I should've realized that." Dante joined Lari, kissing her gently. "Well, let's start tracking this guy then."

Slam and Jaz took the lead, moving quickly, pausing every so often to check the scent. Soon they were in town. "It is getting harder now. His scent is getting lost among others," Slam told them, pausing briefly.

"This way," Dante told him, sniffing the air.

They slowed down, hunting the scent they wanted in among the other scents, sometimes losing it, then finding it again. Eventually they lost it and couldn't find it again. Slam looked at the building they were outside. "I think he is in there."

"Shouldn't we be able to follow his scent to the door?"

"Yes, but there are too many other scents. I think his scent is one of them, but I can't be certain."

Dante walked to the door. "It has a security intercom. So how do we get in?"

Slam looked at the window above the canopy over the entrance. "We can enter through that window."

"What about once we're in there? This is an apartment block. That means it's probably where he lives. We need to be invited in."

Slam looked thoughtful. "I will go in the window and find his scent if it is there. It should be clearer near his own apartment. Then I will come back and tell you which apartment is his. We will think what to do after that."

"Okay. We'll wait across the street."

"Jaz will stay with you. I have told her our plans so far."

"No problem, Slam. I speak Spanish, remember?" Dante told him.

"Si, I forgot. I am so used to translating now for Lari. Sorry." He nodded in the direction of some trees. "Wait over there. You will be concealed. I will be back shortly." He sprung and leaped into the open window, disappearing from view.

"C'mon sweetie," Dante said, taking Lari's hand. "Jaz, ven con nosotros y esperar bajo los árboles."

Once they were concealed under the trees, Dante sighed. "We can't get in there without an invitation." He frowned at the building. "And what are we going to do once we are inside?"

"We can take the camera and compel him to forget what he saw." Lari smiled, leaning her head on his shoulder. "If he doesn't have the camera and he can't remember us, then our problem's solved. Are you afraid Slam wants to kill him?"

"A bit. He says he won't, but I don't know if he's telling the truth." He sighed again. "But we still have the problem of being invited in. How do we get around that? Can we get around that?" Dante stared hard at the building.

"Would be nice if we could just compel him to let us in," Lari interrupted his reverie.

Dante stopped looking at the building and smiled at Lari. "Yeah, it would. But we can't do that."

"Why can't we compel someone to let us in? We can compel them to do all sorts of things."

"Because the invitation to enter must be freely given or it will have no power and we still won't be able to enter," Dante explained to her.

"That's so not fair," Lari pouted. "Does he have to invite all of us in individually? And can he invite us through that intercom or does it have to be at the door?"

"Yes, the invitation must be for each of us, or it must specify us as a group. I think if he invites us through the intercom, then we can enter his apartment."

"Okay. Then I have an idea."

"Go ahead," Dante urged. "Tell us."

"We go to the entrance and buzz his apartment. Then I'll tell him I'm the surfer girl he saw and ask if he'd like an explanation of what he saw. Get him to invite us in."

"How will you get him to invite all of us?"

Lari thought hard. "I'll tell him it needs all of us to explain. To show him how we did it."

"It's worth a shot. I don't know if it'll work or not, but I don't have a better idea." Switching to Spanish, he asked Jaz if she had any alternatives.

She shook her head, "No."

"Then I'm willing to give that a shot."

They waited in the shadow of the trees for nearly five minutes before they saw Slam walk out the front entrance and cross the road to join them under the trees.

"Did you find him?" Dante asked.

"No. I searched the whole building but I could not find his scent. He is not in there."

"Damn. We've lost him."

"We will continue to hunt. Perhaps we will pick up his scent again soon. I suggest we separate. Jaz and I will go in that direction." He pointed down the road they were on. "You and Lari should go that way." He pointed to the side street. "He may have turned the corner. If one of us finds the scent, we will tell the other."

"What if we don't find him, Slam?" asked Lari, looking worried.

"We will. We will find his scent again and discover where he is hiding." He smiled at Lari. "Do not worry."

"'Kay." Lari smiled doubtfully. "C'mon Dante. Let's get back to looking for him." She tugged on his hand and together they sped up, turning the corner and disappearing as Jaz and Slam disappeared down the street.

THIRTY-FOUR

The sun rose and they hadn't found the mystery photographer, having searched all night. Several times they'd found his scent, only to lose it again and again.

"So what do we do now?" Lari asked.

"We will keep looking," answered Slam. "It is likely that he will come out of wherever he is hiding and we will pick up his scent again."

She sighed. "Yeah, I get that part, but what do we do now? We can't leave the Hummer here. So do I drive it into town and park it in some carpark while we keep looking, or do we check in somewhere so I can leave it there?"

"Oh. I am sorry. We must move it if it cannot stay here."

"Dante?" Lari looked at him. "Any suggestions?"

"Carpark. It might be an idea for us to move on once we've got rid of the photos. We can come back again later."

"Okay." She pouted. "I hate this guy, whoever he is. He's messed up my surfing when I finally got to do some." She smiled and sighed. "You all jumping in while I park it?" she asked.

"Sure. Slam, Jaz... jump in."

They all climbed into the Hummer and Lari started the engine. "I'll park it in the first big carpark I see, okay?"

"Sounds good, sweetie," Dante told her.

She drove into town and parked in a large open air car park. Getting out, she asked, "Okay. So where do we start our search today?"

"I don't..." Dante suddenly spun round. "That way! I picked up his scent. He's over that way."

They all turned to face the same direction as Dante. "Yes. That is his scent," Slam agreed with Dante. "We must be careful. It is harder to track in daylight. We should avoid moving at high speed unless we must."

"Let's get after him," Dante suggested.

"Yes. Before he disappears again."

Quickly they all began walking fast in the direction of the scent. It stayed strong but they didn't seem to be getting closer to their target.

"Where is he, Dante? Why aren't we catching up to him?" asked Lari as they rounded another corner.

"I don't know. His scent is still strong, though."

"Yeah, I know... In there! Everyone, stop! He's in there." She stared through the window of a café.

"Are you sure?" Dante asked.

"Yes. I turned my head just to look in there and I got his scent stronger."

"Well. We've found him and we haven't. There's a lot of people having breakfast in that café from the look of it. How will we know which one is him?"

"Dante, you are good at the human things. We will wait out here and you will go in and buy something of whatever it is that humans buy from there at this hour, and while you are inside, you will find the table where he is seated. Just walk around inside and find where the scent is strongest. You can do that, yes?"

"Yeah, I can do that."

"Then we will know who he is and we can wait for him to leave."

Lari looked puzzled. "How come we can't just wait here for him to leave anyway? I mean, aren't we going to get his scent when he leaves?"

"Yes, we could," answered Slam. "But you wish for us to remain unnoticed and I do not think we can stand outside this café unnoticed for any great length of time. Also, while we do not know what he looks like, he has photos of you, Lari, and may also have photos of Dante."

"Then is it smart to send Dante in?"

"Oh, no. I had not thought of that. Tell me what I must buy in there and I will do it. Dante, you and Lari and Jaz please wait over there where you are no longer in direct view of the café."

"Buy a coffee and a donut. Ask for a flat white and a sugared donut."

"A flat white and a sugared donut."

"Yes."

"I can do that. Wait for me over there. I won't be long." Slam walked inside the café while the other three crossed the road and sat in a bus shelter.

Lari leaned her head on Dante's shoulder. "I'm nervous, Dante. Why am I nervous?"

"I don't know. I'm anxious. I don't want anything to go wrong, and before you ask, no, I don't have any idea what could go wrong, but I'm still anxious."

"I wish I could see what Slam's doing. Do you think he's found which table the guy is sitting at?"

"We'll soon find out. Shouldn't be much longer before Slam comes out and joins us."

"What are we going to do once we know who he is?"

"Follow him somewhere less public so we can compel him to hand over the photos?"

Lari grinned. "Okay. Dumb answer to a dumb question."

"Pronto vamos a deshacernos de estas fotos y todos estaremos a salvo de nuevo," Jaz spoke up.

"Si, Jaz," Dante answered her.

"What did she say?"

"She said, soon we'll get rid of the photos and everyone will be safe again."

"Oh, yes, I hope so."

Slam walked out of the café and joined them in the bus shelter. "I found his table. We will wait for him to leave the café now. I will recognize him." An elderly lady walked past the bus shelter. "Excuse me, madam. Would you like this coffee and donut? I am not hungry and would rather it not go to waste." Slam offered her the donut and coffee.

"Why, thank you," she smiled at him, taking the coffee and donut.

"Have a lovely day," he smiled at her in return.

"You too, sir." She continued walking, clutching the coffee in one hand and the bag holding the donut in the other.

"I would never have expected that of you, Slam," Dante told him.

He shrugged. "She reminded me of my mother."

THIRTY-FIVE

Suddenly, Slam seemed more alert. "That is him," he said as a slim man dressed in black jeans, a blue Tshirt and runners walked out of the café. "We shall follow him to somewhere less public."

"Okay," answered Dante as they began to follow behind the man.

"Where's the camera?" asked Lari.

"I did not see it in the café. Perhaps it is wherever he stayed last night."

"His scent isn't as strong," Lari frowned. "I suppose there's a lot of other people around..." She paused before continuing, "If he has the camera at his place, and we can't compel him to take us there and invite us in, how will we get it?"

"That is a good question. I do not have the answer, I'm afraid."

"I do," Dante interrupted with a smile.

"How?" asked Lari.

"What you said before, Lari. You can introduce yourself as the surfer girl from last night and get him to invite you into his place and once you're there, you can find the camera and destroy the photos. After he invites you in, you can compel him to sleep and forget you so he doesn't even remember meeting you."

"Duh, another dumb answer to a dumb question." She grinned at him. "I've gotta stop asking dumb questions or you're gonna start looking too smart."

Slam looked puzzled. "Dumb question? I did not think it was dumb. But it was a very good answer, Dante. And, yes, I think that is what we shall do to get the camera in our possession."

The man they were following turned into a lane. Dante spoke, "Here's our opportunity. Lari, you and Jaz get in front of him to distract him. Slam and I will compel him and get him to go somewhere a bit more discreet."

"I have told Jaz the plan," Slam told them.

"C'mon Jaz," Lari smiled at her. The two girls vanished and reappeared in front of the man.

"What the...? Where the hell did you two come from?" he stopped and asked, startled.

They smiled at him. "From there." Lari pointed behind him to where Slam and Dante were standing.

The man frowned, turning to look where she pointed. "Shit! Who are you guys?" he exclaimed as he saw Dante and Slam.

"We're friends," Dante told him as he compelled him. "You are going to answer some questions for us, but first you will come somewhere more private with us."

"Yes. Friends. I'm going to answer some questions. Let's go somewhere more private," he obediently replied.

"Ask him to take us somewhere we can be alone," Slam told Dante.

"Take us to somewhere private where we won't be interrupted," Dante told the man.

"Yes. I will take you to my home."

"No. No, not your home. Take us somewhere else private."

The man looked confused, frozen where he stood.

"Maybe we should get a room somewhere and take him there. It might be easier," Larissa spoke up.

"We'll get a room. You can come with us," Dante told the man.

"Dante will keep him in thrall. It is harder to do to a human who is conscious so Jaz will assist Dante. You and I will go and find us a room. Somewhere we can take this man to and question him," Slam told Lari.

"Okay... Are you going to wait here with him?" she asked Dante.

"No, they will come with us but remain out of sight while we check in. Dante cannot answer you as he is concentrating on keeping the man in thrall."

"Oh, okay. Thanks for the explanation, Slam. I think I saw a suitable motel when we were trailing his scent to the café."

"We shall try there and hope it is good then," he answered her with a smile. "Dante and Jaz will walk with him a short distance behind us. We do not want anyone to notice the man enter with us."

"And we need to know where the camera is," Lari added.

"Yes, let's find a room."

Lari and Slam walked out of the lane and began walking fast toward the motel Lari had noticed when they were tracking the man. Dante, Jaz and the man followed them a short distance behind, waiting out of sight as Lari and Slam went in to check in.

A few minutes later, Lari and Slam reappeared and walked towards a unit at the back of the complex. Dante, Jaz and the man followed them without being noticed. They all quickly entered and immediately Slam closed all the curtains.

"Now we have privacy."

"Time to answer some questions. What is your name?" Dante asked the man.

"Derek," he answered.

"Sit down, Derek." The man sat down. "Good. You took photos of some surfers last night at Mavericks. Have you told anyone about those photos?"

"No..." Derek frowned as he answered.

"Good. Where is the camera?"

"I don't know," he answered.

Dante frowned. "What do you mean? Have you lost it?"

"No. It's not my camera."

"Ask him what he thinks he saw," Lari interrupted.

"What did you see last night?"

"I was playing WarZone last night. I didn't see anything."

"You were out on the cliffs, taking photos. What were you taking photos of?"

"I wasn't taking photos. I was playing WarZone."

Dante looked disturbed. "He is under compulsion. He cannot lie to Dante," Slam told the room. "I do not understand."

"Do you know who took the photos?" Dante tried a new direction of questioning.

"Yes."

"Tell me who it was that took the photos and tell me what you know of them." Dante was smiling as he finally had some success with his questions.

"Brock. He took photos and a video. He saw a surfer drown who didn't drown."

"Who is Brock?"

"Friend. We play WarZone together."

"Have you seen these photos and the video?"

"Yes."

"Tell me everything you can think of about the photos and the video."

"There was a girl surfing in just a bikini. It's really cold out there but she didn't look cold. There were pictures of her looking drowned under the water after she came off her board, and pictures of her sitting up on her board after they got to shore. Brock took video of the guy pulling her out of the water and putting her onto her board and swimming her back into shore and then her sitting up."

"We must get that video. The pictures can be explained away, but the video is..." Slam shook his head.

"Does Brock have these pictures and video?" Dante asked.

"Yes."

"Has he shown them to anyone else?"

"I don't know."

"Where is Brock?"

"He was at the café with me this morning. Then I left. I don't know where he is now."

"Was he still at the café when you left?"

"Yes."

"He was the only one at the table when I saw him," Slam told them.

"Was Brock always at the table with you?"

"No. He went to the bathroom."

"Oh, damn. We have taken the wrong man... although he knows of these pictures and has seen them and this information he gave us about the video was important. He must come back to the café with us and point out who Brock is." Slam turned to Lari. "Jaz and Dante will remain in control of this man. You and I will control this Brock. Dante must remain concentrating on continuing to compel this Derek, so he won't be able to instruct you. You will follow my instructions, yes?"

She looked at Dante, who nodded. "Yes, I will. Why is it Dante needs to concentrate so hard on compelling Derek and can't talk to me. He doesn't need to work that hard on compelling the people we drink from."

"No. I'm sure he does what we all do and tells them to fall asleep. Then we no longer need to compel them. Derek is awake, and we need him to remain awake. If Dante stops compelling him, Derek will stop being controlled by him."

"Oh, okay. Let's go find this Brock guy then."

"We're going back to the café and you're going to point Brock out to us," Dante told Derek.

"I'm going to point out Brock."

"Yes."

"Let's go," Slam said as he opened the door and they all left to return to the café.

THIRTY-SIX

The café was still busy when they arrived. "Is Brock still here?" Dante asked Derek.

"Yes. He's at that table." Derek pointed to a guy sitting alone at a table with a laptop open in front of him.

"We're going to join him and you're going to tell him not to shout or draw attention to us," Dante instructed him.

"Yes."

"I will compel him, Lari. We will stay a moment at the table. Then we will all leave together and return to the motel. Once I'm compelling him, I won't be able to instruct you. If I look like I'm losing control of him, you need to be ready to take over compelling him until I can regain control. Will you be okay with that?" Slam asked.

"Yeah, I should be," she answered.

They walked over to the table. Brock was so engrossed in his computer that he didn't notice them until they all sat down. He looked up, seeing Derek first. "Hey, you're back." Then he noticed Derek's companions. "Oh shit! You're the... the..."

"Don't shout or do anything to attract attention," Derek told him, as he'd been instructed.

"Yes, Brock. Do not shout or do anything to draw attention to us," Slam compelled him. "We will sit here a moment and then you will come with us."

"I'll come with you."

"Drink your coffee. Finish it," Slam told him. Brock did as he was told. "Put away your computer." Brock closed the laptop, removed a dongle attached to its USB port, and put the laptop into a neoprene sleeve, pocketing the dongle. "Have you paid your bill?"

"Yes."

"Good. We will leave now." Brock, Slam and Lari all stood and walked out.

"We're going to return to the motel now," Dante told Derek and he, Derek and Jaz stood up to leave, following the others out of the café.

They returned to the motel a short walk later. "Sit on the bed," Slam and Dante instructed the two men.

Lari sat on the bed opposite, chewing her fingernails and looking worried. "Uh, guys... what was he doing with that computer?" She stared at the laptop and kept chewing her nails.

"Derek, you will sleep now," Dante instructed him, and Derek fell back onto the bed, immediately asleep. Dante sighed with relief. "That was the longest

I think I've ever had to compel someone." He walked over to join Lari and sat next to her.

"Do you have the photos and video you took last night on the cliffs?" Slam asked Brock.

"Yes."

"Who have you shown it to?"

"Derek and AbeBeTeddy."

"Who?" asked Dante, looking stunned. "Did he say AbeBeTeddy? What kind of name is that?"

"Who is AbeBeTeddy?" asked Slam.

"A guy I play WarZone with."

"Where is AbeBeTeddy?"

"I don't know."

"That's not good," said Dante. "Can we find out?"

"How do we contact AbeBeTeddy?" Slam asked.

"On WarZone."

"Where is the camera you took the photos and video with?"

"At home."

"Ask him if he's deleted the photos and video from the camera, Slam," Dante told him.

"Have you deleted the photos and video from the camera?"

"Yes."

"Are there any copies of these photos and videos?"

"Yes."

"Where are these copies?"

"I emailed them to AbeBeTeddy, and there are copies on my laptop."

"You will sleep now Brock," Slam instructed and Brock fell back beside Derek, sound asleep. "We must find this AbeBeTeddy," he told Dante. "What is this WarZone?"

"Sounds like an online game. Give me his laptop and I'll see what I can find out." Slam handed over the laptop and Dante removed it from the sleeve. "I need that dongle he had in the café. Can you get it out of his pocket, Slam?" Slam reached into Brock's jacket and found the dongle, handing it to Dante.

He loaded the browser and searched for a link to the online game. Finding it, he clicked on it and waited for the log-in screen. "Good. He had his username and password saved, or you would've had to wake him and compel him again, Slam." He chuckled. "You won't believe his username."

Lari leaned over his shoulder. "Oh, that's funny!" she giggled. "He calls himself Bloodsucker." Slam looked puzzled. "People make up names for themselves in the game. That's what he called himself. It's so funny. We're bloodsuckers... I can't stop laughing." Her giggles increased as she pulled faces, trying to stop the laughter.

"Have you found this AbeBeTeddy?"

"Sort of. There's a list of people in his..." He frowned, "They call it a zone list. I think it's the group he plays with... his team, or something... AbeBeTeddy is on that list but it doesn't look like he's online." He frowned as he studied the screen. "Let me find the photos and video on the laptop and get rid of them. I can leave the game open and wait for this AbeBeTeddy to appear online."

"This online game makes no sense to me," Slam told him.

"Don't worry about it. It's too much for me to try to explain... Oh, found the photos... And there's the video..."

"Can I see them before you delete them?" Lari asked, finally not laughing.

"Sure." He tilted the laptop so she could see the screen and opened the photos and then the video.

"Wow. Slam was right. The photos could've been explained away, but that video... wow."

"Yes, and this AbeBeTeddy has a copy. Let's hope he hasn't shared it, and that he doesn't share it." Dante deleted the photos and video. "Well, they're gone from this machine at least."

Derek and Brock chose that moment to wake, both sitting up almost at the same time. Their expressions went from confusion to fear almost immediately. "Help!" Derek called out.

"What the!" cried Brock at the same time.

Slam and Jaz reacted immediately, biting and feeding from them, discarding them on the bed, drained of blood and minutes from death.

THIRTY-SEVEN

"You killed them." Lari was shocked.

"I'm sorry. It was instinct."

"Well, that changes things." Dante closed the laptop and removed the dongle. "We need to leave. We'll take his computer with us so we can try to locate this AbeBeTeddy." He packed the computer into its sleeve and put the dongle in his pocket. "What name did you check in under?"

"I didn't check us in. Slam compelled the desk clerk to give us a room and a key without checking us in."

"That's good. Where's the key?"

"Here," Slam waved it at him.

"Put it on the desk there," Dante told him. Slam dropped the key on the desk. "Okay. Let's work out our next move and get out of here."

"I guess this means we're not going to San Francisco now?" Lari asked sadly.

Dante shook his head. "Sorry, beautiful. I think we need to get a long way from here. We can come back and do San Francisco when we come back here for you to surf again."

"Lake Tahoe? You said we could go there before. Can we go there now, instead?"

Dante nodded. "Yes. Slam, do you and Jaz want to continue with us to Lake Tahoe?"

Slam nodded. "Yes, it would be good for all of us to leave here."

"Okay, let's all walk out of here as if nothing's wrong. We'll go straight to the car and head for Lake Tahoe." He reached across and gave Lari a one-armed hug. "Slam, I know you can drive. Would you mind driving the Hummer so Lari and I can concentrate on trying to find this AbeBeTeddy?"

"Yes, I can drive it, but I do not know how to get to Lake Tahoe."

"I'll program the sat-nav for you." He saw the blank look on Slam's face. "It's a map. It talks to you. It will tell you where and when to turn off and how long the trip should take." Slam still looked confused. "Don't worry. I'll program it. You just follow its instructions."

"Okay. Are we ready to leave?"

"Almost. Their bodies are drained of blood and the fang marks have vanished, but we need to do something..." He got up and searched the kitchenette, finding a steak knife. He tossed it to Slam. "Slash their wrists. They won't know what happened to the blood, but at least they'll think they know how it was drained."

"Dante, are they still alive?" Lari frowned, staring at the two bodies on the bed. "It looks like they're breathing."

"Barely. They can't survive, Lari, and we will not be turning them."

"Oh. Are they... does it... hurt?"

"No. They feel nothing, there is nothing left but a few breaths." He returned to her and gave her a hug. "This is the ugliness that sometimes accompanies being like us. I wish you never had to see this."

She smiled sadly. "It's all my fault. If I hadn't gone surfing last night, this wouldn't have happened."

"Lari, I told you earlier, and I'll tell you again. It's not your fault. You could've come off your board and been knocked unconscious in daytime when there were many more people around to see. Stop beating yourself up over it. It was an accident. Got it?"

She nodded. "I still feel guilty."

"Well, don't." He kissed her gently. "I'll do you a deal. You stop feeling guilty about this and I'll stop feeling bad that you had to see it."

She gave a small laugh. "Deal. But I think it might take a while for all the guilt to go."

"Love you, beautiful," he told her, kissing her again.

"Love you, too," she answered.

"I don't wish to interrupt, but shall we leave now?" asked Slam.

"Yes. Let's go." They all walked out of the room as if nothing was wrong. The two couples held hands as they strolled out of the motel complex and Dante carried the laptop in its sleeve. The desk clerk paused and stared out the window at them as they walked past the entrance, not recognizing them and wondering where they'd come from. None of them noticed him as they crossed the road and walked towards their SUV.

THIRTY-EIGHT

They arrived at Lake Tahoe early in the afternoon. Slam was still driving the Hummer with Jaz in the passenger seat and Dante and Lari studying the computer in the backseat. He pulled into a fuel station.

"Oh, is it fuel time again? Damn, this thing can go through gas," Dante complained, looking up. "Hey, we're in Tahoe." He closed the laptop and handed it to Lari. "I'll fill her up. We should check in somewhere and figure out what we do next." He got out and started fueling up the Hummer.

"Ummmnn, Slam? I didn't feed last night... We were so busy chasing the photographer guy... I'm getting thirsty. Sorry, there must be humans close by... I smelled the blood when Dante got out."

"Oh." He looked across at Jaz, then back towards Lari. "Do you wish to feed from us? Would that ease things for you?"

"No, it's not that bad yet. Thanks. Just get us checked in somewhere soon."

"Yes. I will do that."

"And it's probably best if I don't go in with you while you're checking in... Maybe find somewhere I don't need to walk through a lobby full of people to get to our room."

"Yes."

Dante jumped back into the Hummer. "You're thirsty," he said to Lari. "I can feel your hunger."

"Yes, she has just informed us of this. We will find a motel where she does not need to go through a lobby to get to our room."

"Yeah, good idea."

Slam started the Hummer and drove through town looking for a suitable motel. "This one?" he asked, seeing a motel similar to the one they'd killed the two men in.

"Yeah, it will do. Pull in and I'll check us in."

Slam drove in and parked by the front entrance. Dante got out and disappeared inside, returning a few minutes later. He got back into the SUV. "Okay, drive round the building Slam. I got us a family unit. It's down the back. Last on the right, he said."

"This is a big difference from where we stayed in Hollywood, Dante," Lari told him, her eyes huge as she took in her surroundings.

"Yes. That was at least four stars. This is budget." He grinned. "Maybe two stars if we're lucky." He reached across to hug her. "But it will do as somewhere for you to lay low till it's dark enough to head out and feed."

"And somewhere we can study that computer game and see if AbeBeTeddy logs on."

"That too. This is it, Slam. Room 132. Park in the space out front of it." Slam pulled up in front of the unit and they all got out. "I'll get our bags. You get straight inside, Lari," Dante told her, handing her the room key.

"I will assist," Slam told them. "Ir interior con Lari, Jaz."

Jaz and Lari quickly entered the unit while Slam and Dante collected their baggage and brought it inside. Lari was sitting on one bed with the laptop open, the dongle hanging off the side. Jaz was on the other, reading a book.

"He's online," she told them. "He just said hi to me. He thinks I'm Brock, but he didn't call me that."

"He didn't?" Dante asked her as he joined her on the bed.

"Well, I figure he thinks I'm Brock coz I'm using his account, but he called me Pharaoh, which must be Brock's name in the game."

"Oh, okay. We need to find out where he is."

"Yeah. He's talking about the photos and video Brock sent him."

"I cannot hear anything. How is it you hear him?" Slam asked, sitting on the other bed with Jaz, who stayed absorbed in her book.

"He's not really talking. He's actually typing into the chat window. It's called chatting but it's really typing, and when I say he's talking to me, I mean that he's typing to me," she explained.

"Oh, I think I understand."

"So what's he saying about the photos and video, beautiful?" asked Dante.

"Here, look." She turned the laptop so he could see the screen.

He read out loud, "They're some mad photos you sent me, Pharaoh. That chick looked totally drowned. I would've thought you doctored them or something except you sent that video, too. No way could she hold her breath under there for that long. And if she was faking it, how come that dude came and rescued her? How is she alive? Who are they?"

Lari looked at him. "So what do I answer him?"

Dante shook his head. "I don't know. I'm still absorbing what I read."

"Is there a way they could've been faked? Could I tell him that and see if he believes it?"

"No. I wish it was that easy, but you've seen them. If it was just the photos, I'd say go for it, but that video... there's just no way to explain it."

"He's asking if I'm there."

"Tell him you'll be back in a minute."

She typed. "Done. I told him to hang on."

"Agree with him that they're mad."

"Okay. Yup, totally mad," she said out loud as she typed. She pulled a face as she stared at the screen. "He wants to know who they are and how she's alive. Now what do I say?"

"I don't know."

"Dunno," she said as she typed.

"No! Oh damn, too late. I didn't mean for you to type that," Dante sighed.

"Sorry. I can't take it back."

"I know. It's okay. What did he say?" He leaned over to look at the screen again. "You should post it on the web or sell it to the media, or something," he read out loud. "Oh hell, no. We can't let that happen."

"Dante, I just thought of something."

"What, beautiful?"

"This guy could be anywhere in the world. What if he's not even in America? How do we get the photos and video back?"

"I hadn't thought of that. We just have to go wherever it is we need to. Speaking of that, we need to find out where he is."

"Oooh, he just asked me where the video was made," she exclaimed. "It was made in California," she typed as she spoke. "Where are you?" She paused, staring at the screen. "He answered! He's in Boise, Idaho." She turned to Dante, grinning. "He is in America! Where's Boise, Idaho? Is it far?"

"About four or five hundred miles, I think." Dante smiled. "It's sort of north of here. But we still have to find out where in Boise he is."

"I don't know how to get his address." She frowned, chewing her lip. "Oh, wait! I have an idea." Quickly she started typing again.

Dante leaned over to look at the screen and read out loud what she typed. "I have more video if you want to see it but too much to email. Have you got an address I can send it to?" He grinned at her. "Smart."

"He gave me his address, Dante." She turned the computer so he could see the screen clearly. "Write it down." He grabbed a notepad and pen from the bedside and quickly wrote the address.

"I'll send you the video," she typed. "Gotta go now, talk later."

THIRTY-NINE

As soon as it was late enough, Lari disappeared to feed, returning about forty-five minutes later. "Okay. That's me good now," she told them. "Are we going to stay all night here, or can we start driving towards Boise and AbeBeTeddy now?"

"What would you rather do? It's probably about seven or eight hours drive time. Did you want to have a look around here first?"

She smiled. "I've been for a bit of a run. Think I found that road from the movie... Y'know, the one I told you about." She nudged Dante. "I ran it."

Dante laughed. "Clever. But what about the millions of photos you like to take?"

She pulled her camera from her pocket. "Done. Took it with me."

"Then can we go now?" asked Slam. "I would feel much better once these photos are destroyed."

"Me too," said Dante. "Okay. Toss our bags back in the beast and let's start driving to Boise. Who's doing the driving?"

"I will," Lari volunteered.

"Okay, Lari's driving. You and Jaz are okay in the back, Slam?"

"Si."

"Yes, thank you, Dante," Jaz added in her heavily accented voice.

"Jaz! Your English is heaps better!" exclaimed Lari.

"I understand more also," she added with a smile. "The book I have been reading is to help teach me English."

"Well, you're doing great!" Lari gave her a hug. "Better than I am with Spanish..." She rolled her eyes and grinned.

"You will learn." Jaz smiled and leaped into the back of the Hummer. Slam jumped in beside her and Dante and Lari climbed into the front.

"Ready?" Lari asked, firing the engine. "Want to program that sat-nav thing for me, Dante?" she asked, idling the truck.

Dante turned it on and typed in AbeBeTeddy's address. "Eight hours and twenty minutes according to this. Turn right out of here." He put the sat-nav back in its mount.

"Okay." She drove out of the motel and turned right onto the road. "So, how are we going to get into his house? Or will we get him to come out?"

"I don't know yet, beautiful. We've got eight hours of driving time to think of something. Slam, Jaz, do either of you have any ideas?"

"Not yet, Dante, but let me think on it," answered Slam.

Lari turned east onto the I-80. "Woohoo, nearly two hundred miles down this road before I get to turn off again. We'll need fuel along the way."

"Wherever you want to stop, beautiful. No need to worry about feeding. We're all good." Dante turned to the back. "Slam, do you wanna hand me that laptop of Brock's?" Slam handed it over. "Thanks." Dante put it on his lap and opened it. "Where's the dongle?"

"Ummnn..." Lari concentrated. "Oh, it's in my pocket." She reached into her pocket and handed the dongle to Dante. "Will it work while we're driving?"

"Maybe. Depends on the reception."

"What are you doing?"

"It just occurred to me that we should check Brock's email box and make sure he hadn't emailed those pics to anyone else."

"Oh yeah. Good idea."

He plugged it in and waited. "Damn. Not working. I'll check what else is on his computer... see if there's any other stuff hidden that we might want to get rid of." He studied the machine while he opened and closed files and folders. "No more pictures, but it looks like the only email was sent to AbeBeTeddy... or I think that's him. It's the only email with the photos and video attached."

"How'd you know there was only one email sent with the pics if you can't get online?" Lari asked.

"He keeps logs." He blinked. "Kept logs. I found the logs."

Lari sighed, "Amuse me, Dante... Eight hours is a long drive and I'm bored. It's not like sightseeing coz we can't just wander off and look around."

He grinned at her and put away the laptop. "Amuse you? Give me a minute to think of something."

"Okay, but make it good," she grinned back.

FORTY

It was mid-morning when they reached Boise. They parked about a block away from AbeBeTeddy's house and waited. "So, did anyone come up with any ideas?" Lari asked.

"No," they chorused.

"I could knock on the door and maybe get him to invite me in... but I don't know how the rest of you would get in."

"Lari, that's not a bad idea. Knock on the door and get him to invite you in... then compel him to come out... no, wait... I forgot. You're not as strong as we are." He smiled gently at her pouting face. "You're young, beautiful. That's what I meant. It takes a lot to compel someone who's awake. Compelling him to sleep isn't the same. It was really tough for me when I had to do it." He frowned, deep in thought. "Jaz is strong enough, but her English isn't good enough..."

"What if Jaz and I go together and knock on his door? I can do the talking and Jaz can compel him to obey me. Does she need to know much English to do that?"

"Let me think..." He thought a bit longer. "That might work! Great idea, Lari." He turned to face the back. "Slam, can you teach Jaz enough English that she can compel AbeBeTeddy to obey Lari?"

"Si. We will practice now." He turned to Jaz. "Vamos a practicar algo de Inglés ahora. Repita después de mí, you will obey Larissa."

"You will obey Larissa," Jaz repeated.

"You will not draw attention to us."

"You will not draw..." she broke off, frowning.

"Attention. You will not draw attention to us."

Jaz nodded. "You will not draw attention to us."

"Si. Ahora, lo dicen todo juntos."

"You will obey Larissa. You will not draw attention to us," Jaz repeated in her thick accent.

"That will do. Usted debe mantener el control para Larissa. ¿Se puede hacer esto Jaz?"

"Si."

Slam nodded at Dante and Lari who were watching intently. "Shall we do this then? Jaz will compel him to obey you, Larissa, and keep him quiet. You must direct him to join us here."

In the background, Jaz continued repeating softly, "You will obey Larissa. You will not draw attention to us."

"Could I tell him to invite us in? Would that work? Coz it's not me compelling him."

Slam shook his head. "No, it would not work. The invitation must be freely given. If he is compelled to obey you, then the invitation is not freely given."

Lari shrugged. "Where do I bring him then?"

"Here. Get him in the backseat, between Jaz and Slam. Slam and I will work out what happens next while you and Jaz get him here."

"Okay." She looked at Jaz. "So, are we ready?"

"Jaz, ¿estás listo?"

"Si."

"Jaz is ready. Go and bring him back to us."

"Be safe, Lari," Dante warned her, giving her a quick kiss.

"I will be," she answered him, smiling. "C'mon Jaz. Let's get him."

Jaz smiled and nodded, and the two girls jumped out, walking casually down the street to AbeBeTeddy's house. They disappeared into the gate.

"They're at his door now," Dante told Slam. "Can you hear them?"

"No. I cannot hear anything. They must not be speaking yet or I should hear them."

"Good. I thought the same, but I wanted to check... Oh, I can hear him now. He's answered the door. Lari's telling him to go with them." Dante looked worried.

"It's all right, Dante. He is coming with them. Look!" He pointed and Dante saw them all walking back to the Hummer.

"Oh, good. What are we going to do with him?"

"I will take over compelling him when he gets into this truck. I will ask him where these pictures are."

"What if they're in the house?"

Slam shook his head. "I don't know. This may be difficult."

"Yeah." Dante sighed. "I have an ominous feeling."

FORTY-ONE

"That was tricky," Dante said as Slam got AbeBeTeddy under control in the back.

"Huh?"

"Jaz handed over control of AbeBeTeddy to Slam. For a second no-one was compelling him. It could've gone badly."

"Oh. So, now what?"

"Slam's gonna ask him some questions." He turned to face the back. "Ask him what his real name is, Slam. I don't want to keep calling him AbeBeTeddy."

"Tell me your real name," Slam ordered him.

"Dalton."

"Where are the photos Brock sent to you?"

"At home."

"Are they on your computer?"

"Yes."

"Are they anywhere else?"

"Yes."

"Oh great! I knew this was going to get complicated," Dante moaned.

"Where else are they?"

"On my desk."

"Did you print them?"

"Yes."

"Have you told anyone about these photos?"

"Yes."

"Who did you tell?"

"DramaQueen."

Dante pulled a face. "DramaQueen? It's got to be another player from that game."

"Has DramaQueen seen these photos?"

"No."

"Sleep until I tell you to wake, Dalton," Slam ordered. Dalton fell immediately asleep, snoring loudly.

"Oh, loud... Can you tell him not to snore or is that beyond our powers?" asked Lari.

"Sorry, it is beyond our powers. As Jaz and I are sitting beside him, I can assure you we would do it were it possible." Slam gave Dalton a push, so that his head fell forward onto the back of the front seat and his snoring ceased.

"That worked. Leave him like that," Lari grinned.

"We need to get into his house," Slam told them.

"And we can't compel him to let us in. He won't do it just because we ask," Dante replied.

"Can't you just order him to destroy the photos or bring them to us, or something like that?" asked Lari.

"No." Slam shook his head.

"That's only in the movies, beautiful. What we do is similar to hypnotizing him, but it's not the same. Once he's not under compulsion, his free will returns. We can order him to sleep and release our hold on him, but if he's awake and we release our hold on him, then he won't obey us any more."

She shrugged. "Okay. So how do we get inside his house then?"

Slam spoke up. "We will have to threaten him. Make him fear us."

"How do you plan to do that, Slam?" asked Dante.

"We can show him what we are. Tell him he must invite us in or we will kill him and feed from him."

"And then what happens after?" Lari asked. Slam sighed. She frowned and stared intently at Slam. "Can we compel him to forget?"

"No."

"But we can make people believe all sorts of things..."

"Yes, but to make him invite us in, we must make him fear us. That fear will embed the memory, make it harder to subvert."

"But it can be done, right?"

Slam sighed again. "Perhaps."

"Then if we reveal ourselves to him and scare him into inviting us into his house, one of us has to try to compel him to forget what he saw." Lari was adamant. "I don't want another dead person."

Slam looked at Dante and nodded. "Very well. I cannot see any other way. We must reveal ourselves and scare him into inviting us in. I am the oldest and strongest, so after it is done, I will attempt to compel him to forget."

"Thank you, Slam." Lari gave him half a smile. "What if he won't be scared into inviting us in?"

"Then I am sorry, Lari, but we must kill him."

"How will that help us?" she cried out.

"We can enter the house once he is no longer living."

"Not if it's not his house. Maybe it's his 'rent's house or something," she wailed.

"His 'rents?"

"She means it could be his parent's house, Slam. That is possible. We don't know what the living arrangements are."

Slam nodded slowly. He grabbed Dalton's shoulder and pulled him up, grabbing his face and turning it towards him. "Wake up, Dalton," he told him. Dalton's eyes opened, staring blankly into Slam's. "Who lives in your home with you?"

"No-one."

"Do you rent this home?"

"Yes."

"Good. Go back to sleep until I tell you to wake again, Dalton." Dalton fell back asleep. Slam knocked him forward again before he could start snoring. "We have our answer. If he cannot be convinced to let us in, we must kill him."

Lari sighed. "Dante, promise me that it's a last resort."

"I promise," he told her. "Last resort, Slam."

"Yes. We will try to convince him to permit us to enter. If he will not, we kill him. If he lets us in, after we have entered I will try to compel him to forget." Silently he added to Dante, "I may not be able to do that and may have to kill him after all."

Dante nodded. "I understand," he answered him silently. "There's no other choice. I'm sorry, Lari," he whispered to her as she stared forlornly out the windscreen.

FORTY-TWO

"Okay. We should go somewhere more isolated in case he screams or we have to kill him. Lari, start driving. Head for somewhere outside town... Keep your eyes open for anywhere suitable." Lari drove off and Dante looked intently at their surroundings. "Turn there," he told her after they'd driven about five miles.

She turned down a street and in a short while found herself in a dead end surrounded by open space. "Where are we?" she asked.

"No idea. But you can turn the engine off. This will do."

"All right. Are we ready?" asked Slam.

"Yes." Dante and Lari leaned over the front seats.

"Okay." Slam grabbed Dalton's head and lifted it from the back of the front seat. "Wake up, Dalton," he told him.

Dalton's eyes opened, and he looked around him, confused at first, then scared. "You... you're... how did... help! Help!" he started yelling.

"It will do you no good to yell. There is no-one but us to hear you," Slam told him. "You recognize us, yes?"

"Yes..." Dalton answered him nervously. "Well... no... I don't recognize you but I recognize them in the front." He looked at Lari and Dante. "She's the surfer that Brock took photos of drowned and he's the guy that rescued her."

"Dile que nos dé permiso para entrar, Slam." Dalton spun to look at Jaz at the sound of her voice.

"What did she say?" he asked, looking back at Slam.

"We want you to invite us into your house so that we may recover those photos from you," Slam told him.

"No way! Why do you..." his voice trailed off.

Slam gave half a laugh. "We insist that you invite us."

"How come you didn't just barge in?" he demanded.

"You saw the photos, Dalton. You know that Lari did not drown, no matter what it looked like. She cannot drown." He smiled. "Do you really want to know what we are?" He nodded. "I see you do." He gave another half-laugh. "You have heard of vampires, Dalton? That is what we are. If you do not give us permission to enter your home and take back those photos, we will kill you. Do you want to know how we will kill you, Dalton? We will feed from you and drain you of blood. It will be very painful and unpleasant. It does not have to be like that, but we would make it so."

"Wh... wh... I..." he stammered. "No!"

"Your friends, Brock and..." he looked at Dante.

"Derek," Dante told him.

"Yes, Brock and Derek... they are already dead. Are you sure that you wish to join them?"

"You did that?"

"Yes. We killed them and we will kill you, unless you invite us into your house. Please say the words, Dalton, and we will go straight there."

He gulped. "I... if I do that, you'll just kill me after."

"No. If I kill you now, I don't need your invitation. Invite us into your house and I will make you forget that you ever met us or saw the photos."

"You won't kill me?" he asked.

"No. Are you going to invite us, Dalton? Just nod yes, if you are."

Dalton gulped again and nodded.

"Good." Slam smiled at him, compelling him again. "You will sleep again until I tell you to wake." Dalton promptly fell asleep again. "Drive back to his house, Lari. He will give us permission to enter."

FORTY-THREE

They drove back to his house, parking out the front this time. Slam lifted Dalton's head again. "Wake up, Dalton."

"Huh... uh..." his head swung from one direction to another. "Oh, it wasn't a dream."

"No. We are going to get out and walk to your front door, where you will invite us in."

"I... could just yell, or something..."

"I could kill you in less than thirty seconds." Slam smiled at him. "Shall I?"

Dalton shook his head. "I'll invite you."

"Good." Slam got out and reached for Dalton. "Please get out. I am not a patient man."

Jaz gave Dalton a shove and he got out, standing next to Slam. Jaz quickly followed him out. Lari and Dante hopped out, joining them on the sidewalk.

"Okay, everybody's out. Let's get inside, then," Dante told them.

Slam and Jaz walked either side of Dalton, while Lari and Dante brought up the rear. Reaching the front door, they all stopped. "Invite us," Slam told him.

"I invite you," Dalton blurted.

"All of us, please. Dante, Lari, Slam and Jaz."

"I invite Dante, Lari, Slam and Jaz into my house," he droned.

"Thank you, Dalton. That wasn't so hard, was it?" Jaz opened the front door and they all walked inside. "Show us where your computer and the photos are," Slam told him.

"Here." Dalton gestured to a closed door.

Lari opened the door and walked into the room. A big desktop computer dominated the room. The photos were stacked on the desk beside the keyboard.

"Go sit over there," Slam instructed Dalton, pointing at the chair by the computer. Dalton quickly ran across to the chair and sat.

Slam stayed by the door while Jaz and Dante joined Lari by the desk. "Are these all the photos?" Dante asked him.

He nodded. "Yes."

Dante scooped them up. "Log into your computer and delete them from your hard drive."

Dalton quickly turned the computer on and started typing. He found the folders containing the photos and deleted them.

"The video, too," Dante added, noticing that it hadn't been removed.

Dalton deleted the video.

"Okay. We're going to take these and we're going to make you forget." Dante shoved the photos into his back pocket. "Slam." He nodded at Dalton.

Slam walked over to stand in front of Dalton. "You are going to forget us. This never happened. There were never any photos."

Dalton stared up at him, still fearful. "When does it happen?" he asked.

Slam sighed. He looked across at Dante, silently telling him, "It's not working. He's too scared. I will have to kill him."

Lari looked from Slam to Dalton and back again. "Keep trying..." she pleaded.

"What do you mean, keep trying? Was that it? I didn't forget." His voice got more and more panicked.

Slam tried again. "Look at me, Dalton. Nowhere else. Focus on me." Dalton stared at him. "You are going to forget us. We were never here. There were never any photos."

Dalton's breathing got more ragged. "It didn't work!" He started crying. "I won't tell... I won't... don't kill me... please, don't kill me..." He got louder. "Please don't... I won't... Help! Help!" he began shouting.

Slam moved quickly, grabbing him, biting his neck and drinking. Dalton's shouts subsided into whispers as the blood drained. Slam tossed the limp body back onto the chair.

Remembering Dante's efforts to deflect investigations into how Brock and Derek died, Slam reached for a letter opener on the desk and slashed Dalton's throat. "I am sorry, Lari. It was unavoidable," he told her. Frowning, he realized there was sounds coming from elsewhere in the house. "What is that noise?"

Lari shook her head at Slam. Jaz reached over and hugged her. "Se va a estar bien, Lari. Slam no tuvo otra opción," she consoled her.

"I want to cry, but I can't," she moaned.

Dante walked out of the room and down the hall towards the noise. "Come here! Everyone! Come here!"

They all quickly ran to join him. He was standing in the living room in front of a big screen television. "What is it?" asked Slam.

"We need to get out of here and fast. And baby, I'm sorry, but we're going to have to get rid of your Hummer."

"What?" asked Lari, her sadness at Dalton's death forgotten.

"Look at the news."

They all watched and listened to the news on the TV. "Oh, Dante! They know Brock and Derek are dead! They're saying they were murdered. Someone saw us leave the motel in California... and they saw us get into the Hummer and drive away! They're looking for us."

"Yes, baby. And they got the plate number."

"Can't we just get new plates?"

"They'll be stopping any blue Hummer like yours, whether the plates are different or not." He sighed. "We're getting out of America. Canada isn't too far away. We'll go there." He turned to look at Jaz and Slam. "I'd advise you to get out of America too. They had pretty good descriptions of us all."

"We will come with you to Canada."

"Okay." He stared thoughtfully at the television. "They don't know we're here yet. It said they were still looking in California, but that will change. We'll take the Hummer and get out of here. But we have to find another vehicle and leave your Hummer behind, Lari."

She sighed sadly. "Okay. C'mon, let's go." She thumped the wall as she walked out. "What a shitful day," she muttered. Dante, Slam and Jaz followed her out silently.

FORTY-FOUR

In silence, they all got into the Hummer. Dante immediately began tapping information into the sat-nav. "Route 95 will take us to Canada, Lari. Follow the instructions from this," he told her as he put it back into its mount. Lari looked at him and nodded, still looking unhappy. She started the engine.

"I am very sorry, Larissa. I know that you did not want another dead human," Slam told her as they drove away. "It was truly unavoidable."

Lari pressed her lips together and her eyes flashed. "Not now, Slam. Try explaining later. She's angry and upset. Let her cool down a bit," Dante told him silently.

"How long before I have to give up my Hummer?" she asked Dante.

"A while, baby. The report said they were looking for us in California. It won't be until they discover..." he paused, searching for a way to avoid mentioning Dalton. Sighing he continued, "...that we're in Idaho, that we need to worry more... If we're lucky, we'll get really close to Canada before we need to ditch it."

"How long before we reach Canada?"

"Hours and hours and hours... A very long drive."

"Okay." She looked a little less tense. "It's really not fair that I have to give up my Hummer..." she pouted. "And it's not fair that I really want to cry and I can't. Why can't I cry?"

Dante gave her half a smile. "I don't know why. But none of us can."

"Well, it's wrong. I'd feel better if I could cry... So... Nobody talk to me for a while till I feel better."

"Okay, beautiful," Dante told her, reaching across to give her a one-armed hug.

They drove in silence for nearly a hundred miles before Lari decided she was ready to talk. "Slam, I understand that you did what you had to. I'm not mad at you, really. I'm mad at me, coz all of this happened coz I went surfing and that guy took those photos."

"It's not your fault, Lari," Dante told her.

"No, it is not," added Slam.

"Shut up, both of you. It is my fault and I'm upset that I have to give up my beast. I just don't want to do that. I thought I'd have it for ages and I've hardly had it any time at all." She sighed. "But Dante will buy me something else now, won't you, Dante?" she smiled sadly at him.

"Yeah, I will. What do you want me to get you?"

She shrugged. "Don't know. I'll see what I like the look of and tell ya." She frowned slightly. "What will we do with our stuff when we ditch the Hummer?"

"Depends when and where we have to ditch."

"May I say something?" Slam asked.

"Go ahead, Slam," answered Dante.

"If we are able to drive this vehicle almost to Canada, we should leave it some distance from the border, so that anyone following us does not think to look in Canada."

"Good point, Slam." Dante looked at Lari. "Okay, let's say we can drive this most of the way there... We'll stop and leave the Hummer at least sixty or seventy miles from the border and not on Route 95 either. We'll ditch it on some side road or similar, but well hidden. We'll each take a surfboard and a duffel and run some distance away. At least ten miles. Then we can steal a vehicle and drive closer to the border. We'll dump that vehicle about ten miles from the border and cross on foot. Is that okay with everyone?"

"Yeah," answered Lari.

"Si," answered Slam and Jaz.

"You are better now, Lari?" asked Jaz.

"Yeah, thanks, Jaz. Your English is getting really good."

"Thank you." She paused, concentrating hard. "Slam is helping me... he is telling me the right words. In my head, he is telling me." She smiled.

"Well, it's still good, Jaz." Lari grinned back at her in the mirror. "Okay, I'm in a better mood now... Someone talk about something... And not Idaho or California or anything related to that."

FORTY-FIVE

At Sandgate, about sixty miles from the border, Lari pulled over. "Dante, you take over driving. I don't want to do this."

"Okay." They both hopped out and changed seats.

Dante started the engine and took the next exit from Route 95. He randomly made more turns until they were on an isolated road some distance from where they started. He drove the Hummer slowly into a stand of trees off the side of the road. They all got out and removed the bags and boards.

"Oh, get my iPod... It's hooked up to the stereo," Lari told Dante, who was still leaning inside the Hummer. He reached across and grabbed it, disconnecting the sat-nav and taking that also. He got out and handed the iPod and sat-nav to Lari.

"Anyone got anything else in there?" he asked. "Don't leave anything behind."

"No," answered Slam. "Jaz and I have only these duffels."

"Yeah, that was it for me, Dante," Lari told him.

"Okay. Good. Cover it with branches and stuff... so it's harder to see from the road." Dante looked back towards the road. "I think it's far enough away that it'll be a while before it's noticed, but..." He grabbed some branches and scattered them over the Hummer's roof. The others did the same. Pretty soon it was mostly covered. "Okay, time to go. We're east of Route 95 now, so let's run west."

They each picked up a duffel and a board and ran west, following Dante. Six miles after they crossed Route 95, Dante slowed to walking pace, the others following his lead. "Dante?" asked Lari.

"Time to find a car to steal," he told her. "Look for an easy one... And nothing flashy... Something that won't get noticed fast."

"Like that?" Lari asked, pointing at a Dodge parked on the street ahead.

"Too new. Too hard to hotwire... and nowhere for the boards to go," he answered.

"This one," Slam told them. Dante and Lari stopped and turned round to face him. Slam and Jaz were already inside a red dual cab pickup truck, the two boards they'd been carrying and their duffels deposited in the tray. Dante and Lari joined them, putting the boards and their duffels in the tray and getting in the back seat. "Sorry, I did not think you would mind if I drove," Slam told them as he drove back towards Route 95.

"No, it's good, Slam. Would you like to connect the sat-nav?"

"We just drive down Route 95 until we're ten miles from the border?" he asked.

"Yeah," answered Dante.

"Then no, I do not need it."

"Okay."

"One thing, Dante..."

"Yes?"

"I think ten miles is too close. We should leave this a bit further than that."

"Okay..." He paused, thinking. "Twenty miles sound far enough?"

"Yes. That is better."

"Okay. Drive another thirty or forty miles and we'll ditch this there."

"And we will leave this away from Route 95 when we stop, yes?" he asked.

"Yeah. Same as we did with the Hummer, but we won't hide it off-road unless there's no choice. Try and find a street similar to where we found it to dump it."

"Okay," answered Slam.

"Where are we going when we get to Canada?" Lari asked.

"I don't know. I've been to Vancouver before, but never to this part of Canada," replied Dante.

"Where is this part of Canada?" she asked, laughing.

He grinned. "Somewhere pretty remote that I've never been to. I don't know exactly."

"So how do you know it's remote then?"

"Okay. I don't. It's a crossing I've never done and Vancouver's nowhere near it and that's the only place I know in Canada."

"Do you have a place for us to go to?"

"No." He paused and thought. "We should find somewhere to hide out, though. Better if we don't check into any hotels or motels in case they give our descriptions to the Canadians."

"So where will we go then? Will we just keep moving?"

"No. Let's see if we can find an empty house... A holiday home that no-one's using would be the best."

"Will there be any of those in the part of Canada we're crossing into?"

"I don't know. Let's hope there are."

"Do we steal another car on the other side of the border or are you going to buy me one?"

"We'll steal one to start with. When we figure out what we're doing next, we'll work out buying a new car for you."

Lari shook her head. "Damn, Dante... You're turning me into a car thief." She grinned at him and winked. "Don't look so panicked! I'm teasing you. You never get it when I tease you."

He chuckled. "Baby, I feel bad about all of this."

"Yeah, I got dibs on that. Get in line." She grinned. "I'm over it now. Really. Hummer's gone. Canada's ten minutes into our future. I'm not looking behind."

He shook his head. "Amazing. How can you do that?"

She shrugged. "I don't know. When do we go back to Roswell or is that out of bounds for ages again?"

"Out of bounds. All of America's out of bounds until the heat is gone and I'm willing to risk being there."

"Lucky we locked up good, then," she told him. "Hey, Dante, I just realized something."

"What?"

"You had power in the house when we arrived and there's always been power there... How was that?"

"It was never disconnected. It's automatically paid. It'll stay connected and the bills will stay paid."

"Wow. Is that the same for your house in England or wherever it is?"

"Yes."

"Cool."

Slam turned off the highway just after they passed through Bonners Ferry. He drove down a few more streets, each one seemingly more isolated. "Will this do, Dante?" he asked.

"Yeah, looks fine." They all got out and collected the bags and boards from the tray. "Okay, walk down the street till we're out of sight of anyone who may have seen us... Actually, walk back the way we came in. That way if anyone sees us and connects us to the manhunt, they think we were heading away from Canada."

"Who would see us? Is there any houses here?" Lari asked. "Oh, yes, there is... One house. It's all the way up the other end of the street... But I suppose if there's only one house, we'd be the most excitement around here all day."

"Just walk," he told her.

"Paranoid," she muttered. "And don't we need to run across the border?" Lari asked, frowning.

"Yeah, we'll do that, but away from this truck."

She sighed petulantly, "Oh, okay."

"You can be impossibly grumpy and argumentative," he told her in frustration. Lari pulled a face at him and stuck out her tongue.

They walked to the end of the street and turned the corner heading further away from Route 95. Once they were no longer in sight of the street where they'd parked the truck, Dante told them, "Running time. Go to Route 95, stay close to the road, but not too close, and head north. We need to stay out of sight of the border police too, so don't slow down crossing the border and stay at least ten feet from them so they're not even aware of you. And when we cross the border, we should keep about six to ten feet or more between us as well."

"We know this, Dante," Slam told him.

"I'm explaining for Lari," he replied.

"Oh, I see. Sorry."

"It's okay. Everyone ready?" he asked. They all nodded. "Then, run!" He immediately took off towards Route 95 with Lari, Jaz and Slam following fast behind him.

FORTY-SIX

Not long after they'd abandoned the pickup truck, they were across the border and in Canada. They all came to a stop about fifteen miles inside the border, off-road and hidden in a stand of trees.

"This is a remote area, Dante," Slam told him.

"Yeah, looks like that," Dante answered.

"I don't like our chances of finding a car to steal."

"No. Me either."

"I know that Lari does not like it when humans die at our hands, but the only way I see for us to get a car is to take one forcefully from someone. That would necessitate killing them," Slam told Dante silently.

"What if we could compel them to forget seeing us?" he answered Slam, also silently.

Slam nodded. "I can try. But as before, if it is not possible..."

"Okay. I'll keep Lari here. You go to the road and see what you can do. Try not to kill anyone, please."

"It's very quiet around here and you two are staring intently at each other. Is there a private conversation going on that I'm missing out on?" Lari asked, looking at each of them.

Dante looked at her and smiled. "Yeah, there was. Slam is going to the highway to see if he can find someone with a suitable car or truck and compel them to give it to us."

"Compel them to give it to us?" she asked. "I don't understand."

"He'll do the same as when we feed... compel them to sleep and forget us, y'know, like a dream or something... and then he'll take their car or truck and we'll use it."

"Where will he leave them sleeping?"

"Side of the road? Where they won't be discovered too fast or run over."

"What about bears and things? Are there bears or other wild animals around here that might maul them?"

"Lari!" He sighed and shook his head. "Would you rather Slam kill them and take the vehicle?"

"No."

"Then stop asking questions I don't know the answers to. Slam will find us a car. He won't kill whoever's car it is, and we'll use it to get a long way from here."

Jaz reached for Lari's hand. "It is okay, Lari. He will not kill more humans," she said in her halting English.

Lari smiled nervously at Jaz. "Are you sure?"

"Si. Yes. He will not kill them."

Looking at Dante, Lari told him, "I'm sorry, Dante. I won't ask anymore, okay."

He smiled. "Thank you, beautiful." He turned to Slam. "Okay. Find us a car or pickup truck or something similar." Silently he added, "And please try not to kill whoever has it."

"Lari, will you help me with English?" Jaz asked Lari as she stared after Slam as he disappeared in the direction of the highway.

"Go on, he could be a while. Practice English with Jaz," Dante told her.

She glared at Dante. "I know what you're both trying to do. You want to distract me from worrying that Slam's gonna kill more people." She sighed. "I guess I can't do anything about it." She sighed again. "Okay. But you'd be better helping Jaz learn English since you can speak Spanish and I can't."

"We both will," Dante told her and the three of them sat down together.

Forty minutes later, Slam returned. "I have a pickup similar to our last one," he told them. "It is about five miles from here, parked in the trees."

"What happened to its owner?" asked Lari.

"Alive. Unconscious. I left him at the side of the road near where he stopped for me. He will not easily be seen and he is safe from being run over, also. Last thing he will remember is drinking too much." Slam smiled. "I was lucky. He had alcohol on his breath and it was an easy task to compel him."

Lari smiled. "Thanks for not killing him."

Slam shrugged. "It was not necessary to do so."

They all followed him to the pickup truck. "Won't he wonder what happened to his truck?" Lari asked as they reached it, threw their bags and boards into the tray and climbed in.

"Perhaps. But his last memory will be of walking out of the bar. He will not recollect getting into his truck, so he will think it was stolen from the bar." Slam started the truck and drove further down Highway 3.

"There was a bar around here?" Dante asked.

"It was in his memory."

"You read his thoughts."

"Yes, as he drove toward me. He was thinking about returning to the bar instead of his wife."

Dante and Lari both grinned. "Well, if it was a long way from here, he'll wake up amazed at how far he managed to walk in his state," Lari laughed.

FORTY-SEVEN

They drove for two hours, ditching the stolen pickup truck in Castlegar and stealing another on the outskirts of town. Around an hour and half later they ditched that pickup in Grand Forks, finding and taking another on their way out of town. Reaching Oliver two hours later, they finally found an empty holiday house. Quickly they unloaded the bags and surfboards. Slam broke into the house, opening the front door for them. Lari and Jaz took the bags and boards inside, while Dante and Slam took the pickup and drove away to leave it somewhere well away from where they intended to stay.

Slam returned nearly an hour later without Dante. "Where's Dante?" Lari asked him immediately.

"He has gone to find out information."

"What information?"

"If they are hunting for us here... If we have made the news here... Who owns this house and if they will return to it soon..." He shrugged. "Information."

"Okay," she said unhappily.

"He will return soon. When he does, we must decide what we do next."

"Yeah, okay."

Dante walked in. "Hey."

Lari leaped on him and hugged him.

He laughed as he held her. "What's this for?"

"Coz I love you." She kissed him and released her grip.

"Good. I love you, too." He tossed some newspapers on the breakfast bar. "Now, the good news. They're not looking for us here. We haven't even made the papers. So we have a bit of time to make our next moves."

"Oh, that's great!" exclaimed Lari. "I was starting to feel really down being on the run like that."

"Technically, I think we're still on the run," he told her.

"Yeah, well... I felt... hunted... okay?"

"Yeah. I understand, Lari. I feel better that we're not the targets of a manhunt here, too." Dante sat in one of the armchairs. "This place is only used by its owners in the summer so we're right here for a while."

"It's a really nice place," Lari said, looking around. "It's really modern. I love all the timber and it's so open inside... and the windows... what do they call those windows up there?" She looked up, half-frowning. "Cloister? No... Cl... Clerestory, that's it... They're cool. It feels like it fits into the surrounding area... like it's part of it."

"Yeah, it does feel like it fits in to the surrounding area. But, beautiful, you like it coz it's modern, and you said you liked my house in Roswell coz it was old and gothic... I don't get it."

"I like them both." She grinned. "I like old and modern... Just not boring like my 'rent's house."

He shook his head. "Okay, I get it now. Enough architecture. What are we going to do next?"

"Jaz and I would like to have a look around Canada. We have never been here. Then I think it is time for us to return to our boat in Mexico."

"No suggestions, Lari?"

She shook her head. "I think it's good that they're not looking for us here yet, but they probably will when they can't find us in America, won't they?"

"Yes. I shouldn't think it would be too long before they shared our descriptions with Canada. Perhaps it's time for us to go our separate ways. After all, they'll be looking for four of us, not two."

"I agree," Slam told him. "Perhaps our looking around Canada will be limited to what we can see on our way to Mexico. You are probably right that they will share our descriptions with the Canada officials before too long."

"Yeah." He sighed. "So, Lari, where shall we go?"

Before Lari could answer, Slam spoke. "Jaz wishes me to tell you that you are both welcome to join us in Mexico."

Lari smiled, "Thank you!"

"But we'll say no for now. I'd really like to get to a different part of the world, I think," Dante told them. "Thanks for the offer. Maybe we can see you there another time?"

"You will be welcome," Slam told him.

"So where will we go, Dante?" asked Lari.

"How about Europe? Would you like that?"

Her eyes grew wide. "Europe? Oh, yeah! That would be great! How will we get there?"

"Come with us to Mexico and then we will take you to Spain in our boat. From there you can travel to any part of Europe you wish to and no-one will be looking for you in Spain," Slam invited them.

"Lari? What do you think? Slam's offer sounds good to me."

"Me, too. When do we go?"

"I would like if we could feed before we leave for Mexico. So, would one week from now be too long to wait around here?" asked Slam.

"No. Not too long. One week, it is," replied Dante.

"Yayayayayay!" cheered Lari, dancing around excitedly. "We're going to Mexico and Spain and Europe and we're going on Slam and Jaz's boat! Is it a big boat? A sailboat? Powerboat? I've never been on a boat."

"It is a hundred-foot motor yacht," answered Slam. Seeing the confusion on Lari's face, he continued, "It is called a yacht but it is powered by engines."

"Wow. So cool. I can't wait to see it."

"Hope you don't get seasick since you've never been on a boat," Dante told her wryly.

"Do vampires get seasick?" she asked.

"No. My turn to tease you." He grinned at her.

She pulled a face and stuck her tongue out at him, then laughed. "Oh, I'm so excited! How do we get to Mexico?"

"I'll buy a car before we leave here. I've had enough stolen pickups," Dante said.

"Good. This isn't my replacement for the Hummer, though, Dante... Okay?"

He chuckled softly, "Not your replacement for the Hummer. No, this is just transport from here to Mexico. I'll buy you a replacement for the Hummer when we get to Europe. How's that?"

"Deal." She launched herself onto his lap. "I love you, Dante Hill. Life hasn't been dull since you changed me."

"No, it certainly hasn't."

"We aren't going back through America, though. How will we get to Mexico?" Dante wondered out loud.

"We will buy passage on a boat going to Mexico," Slam told them. "It is how Jaz and I would return there. There are always boats willing to take passengers without many questions."

"That's what we'll do then. How long will we stay in Mexico before we go to Spain, Slam?"

"We can leave almost immediately. Our boat is always ready for departure."

"Great." He nuzzled Lari's ears. "I love you, Larissa. I love how you've adapted so well."

She stared into his eyes, a smile playing across her face. "I love you, too... Forever, my immortal."

THE END

www.ingramcontent.com/pod-product-compliance
Lightning Source LLC
Chambersburg PA
CBHW071308130626
46556CB00004B/1526